I0537484

Hidden

The New Orleans Temptation Series
Part 2

By:

Monica May

ISBN-13:978-0-692-47369-6

Copyright

CONTENTS

Acknowledgments 5

1 Chapter 6-17

2 Chapter Pg 18-23

3 Chapter Pg 24-27

4 Chapter Pg 28-36

5 Chapter Pg 37-48

6 Chapter Pg 49-65

7 Chapter Pg 66-72

8 Chapter Pg 73-80

9 Chapter Pg 81-89

10 Chapter Pg 90-105

11 Chapter Pg 106-109

12 Chapter Pg 110-115

13 Chapter Pg 116-128

14 Chapter Pg 129-144

15 Chapter Pg 145-158

16 Chapter Pg 159-172

17	Chapter	Pg 173-187
18	Chapter	Pg 188-196
19	Chapter	Pg 197-199
20	Chapter	Pg 200-205
21	Chapter	Pg 206-209
22	Chapter	Pg 210-214
23	Chapter	Pg 215-221
	Epilogue	Pg 222-224
	About the Author	Pg 225

ACKNOWLEDGMENTS

A special thanks to my PA Alicia Marietta who works tirelessly to help me do whatever I ask of her simply for the love of helping an Indie Author that she loves so much. Without you, I would not have been able to do blogs, cover reveals, or release parties. Thanks for always bringing me back to reality when I have a freak attack.

I also want to give a big shout out to my Bayou Bitches. Ya'll are amazing and without your shameless pimping my book would go nowhere. Hugs and kisses to all of you as I am so thankful to have you.

And without Kelly Hartigan, my editor, this book would be a pure mess. You rock, Kelly.
http://editing. xterraweb.com

And for the amazing cover, I give props to Beth with Cover It Up Designs. She did an amazing job helping me design a cover that is unique to Hidden but fits The New Orleans Temptation series. I look forward to working with you again soon.
https://www.facebook.com/coveritupdesigns?__mref=me ssage

CHAPTER 1

Great Aunt Gertrude, New Orleans 1949

Smoke fills the air as I walk through the club. Sexy jazz music bounces off the walls as I ascend the stairs. The smell of sex hits me when I reach the top making my own arousal increase. As the owner of the club, I make it my own rule not to mix with the patrons. I have to admit at this moment, I HATE THAT RULE! It's the most difficult rule to follow.

I scan the room watching my girls sway beautifully to the music just out of reach from the exclusive club members that are having sex below them. I pause at the landing to see how far I've come as I look across the large room. The war is over and the ships no longer stop in New Orleans weekly. Boy, those were the days, every weekend 1,500 new sexy young sailors being dumped into the heart of the city at the Port of New Orleans.

I think back to two years ago when I was almost broke. The million my parents left me was dwindling down to nothing. I was desperate to make my burlesque club work.

After taking a trip with one of my many sailors of the week to Vegas, I discovered the world of sex clubs. A world I had no idea existed. This was unheard of; no such club had existed publicly that I was aware of in New Orleans. So why not? I figured I would give it a try. What did I have to lose? And here I stand two years later and this place is a hit!

My club is beautiful, clean, and the atmosphere is uninhabited. I look at the clock to see its almost 2:30 a.m. We never close but it does tend to get almost completely empty between 2:00 a.m. and 4:00 p.m. Taking in the view, my eyes are drawn to the group near the bar. This type of club is extreme for today's time and to see a threesome is even more rare. I try to look away but I can't. There's a young man on his back with a blonde woman kneeling between his legs with his cock in her mouth. She has a firm grasp on his shaft while she moves her hand up and down in sync with her mouth. His beautiful hard length glistens in the low light. An older gentleman stands behind her entering her slowly but firmly from behind. They catch me watching and motion for me to come over. Oh, how I really would love to squat over that young man's face and have him lick my sexual tensions away. But I'm forced to smile politely and wave them off. *Tell me again why I made that stupid rule?*

Finally reaching the back of the room, I brace my arms on the bar for support and look down at Sam's large strong hands as they clean glasses. "Could you be a dear and pour me something stiff, anything," I say, feeling the unrelenting desire between my legs. When he doesn't respond, I look up to see if he's heard my request. I find him gazing down at me with lust.

"Gertie, you look beautiful tonight. Actually, you look beautiful every night, but tonight you are absolutely stunning."

I feel a warm rush of need pulse over my already aching body. His comments surprise me; he has never seemed interested in me before. Always nose to the grindstone doing what he is supposed to do. "Thanks, Sam, you don't look too shabby yourself. Now how about that stiff drink? I really need one fast before I rethink my no play with the patrons rule; this is torture," I huff, looking up at the celling.

"I don't recall you having a no play with your employees rule. Why don't we go make use of that room in the back?" He points to the private room I have for patrons that don't want to be in public but still be a part of the atmosphere. "I've had something stiff in my pants all night watching you."

I'm pleasantly surprised by his response and look up at him with a sinful grin. "Sam, I had no idea you were interested in playing," I say with a sexy tilt of my head as I start to mindfully twirl my hair around my finger. Sam is a guy I never went after because I assumed he was a good boy. He's a rule follower, and I never saw an interest from him.

"Gertie, a man can only watch sex around him all night for so many hours without wearing out his palm during cigarette breaks." He grins down at me.

I saunter behind the bar, and Sam doesn't make a move. I push up against his body and put one hand on his tight ass squeezing as I bend down to reach for the bar closed sign from underneath. Sam and I don't speak as I grab his hand pulling him toward the private room. Locking the door behind us, I lock eyes with his sexy gaze and let him watch me undress button by button. He's drooling by the time I'm naked. He is ten years my junior and could pass for James Dean. Looking down at a very large bulge, I don't hesitate to get his pants off while he quickly discards his shirt. I paw at him with an urgent and needy desire.

"I have never met a woman like you, Gertie. You exude sex and make no apologies for it. I have wanted to be deep inside of you since the day you hired me six months ago," he grunts, smashing his lips on mine and pressing his warm tongue into my waiting mouth.

I push his underwear down to see what he has to offer me. "Sam, Sam, Sammy, why have you waited so long to show me this beautiful thick cock of yours?"

He pulls my waist toward him and my center collides with his rock hard erection grinding it.

"I had no idea you would be interested in a kid like me," he says shyly.

"Only a fool of a woman would not have sex with a man like you. Give me what you have and give it to me good and hard."

"Yes, ma'am, whatever you say."

I chuckle; he is going to play the sexy schoolboy abiding by the teacher's rules. He picks me up by my ass, putting me down onto his length and pressing me against the door with force. I wrap my legs around his waist as he slides into my wetness welcoming his presence.

I moan his name as he brings me to the brink of orgasm, and then he slows down. "Not so fast, ma'am, I want you to feel every slow inch of my cock," he says as we both look down at him entering me slowly over and over. It's so erotic to watch his cock move in and out of my pussy covered in my excitement. The view pushes me over the edge, and I whimper in pleasure as Sam picks up the pace thrusting through my orgasm and finding his own release.

"Oh, Sam, that's wonderful, please don't stop."

"I have no intentions of stopping any time soon!"

And he didn't. Sam and I made love in that locked room until the cleaning crew came in around 6:00 a.m. Sam and I used each other's bodies that night as a release from all the sexual tension of the workday. This became a regular occurrence for us on the shifts we shared, and it was absolutely amazing.

New Orleans – Present Day

Samantha

Setting Aunt Gertrude's diary down, I think, *This may be harder than I expected.* With Phillip gone, I've sworn off relationships. It's been a year and a half since the accident, and I can't say I miss him, which makes me sad. Sad that I have never had what Shelby and Grant have. Phillip and I loved each other in our own way. He helped me get over my first husband cheating by exploiting my need to be sexually experienced. And now that's all I have to go on, outrageous sex! What the hell is wrong with me? I know true love is not out there, yet the wild sex is starting to feel empty without feelings behind it.

The ringing of my desk phone breaks me from my pity party.

"Yes?"

"Ms. Champagne, your eleven o'clock interview is here."

"Please tell him to come on back, thanks."

Moments later, there's a knock at my office door. "Come in," I yell while rustling through the stack of résumés on my desk trying to find my 11:00 a.m. appointment. When I look up from my desk, I see the most beautiful male specimen I have ever seen. He's tall with dark, thick hair long enough to run my fingers through but short enough to still look professional. His eyes are black as coal with thick lush lashes. The caramel-colored skin exposed on his arms makes me want to lick him. And the muscles ... they are just right, not too bulky but perfect.

"Ms. Champagne, I'm sorry, did I catch you at a bad time? You look a bit lost in your thoughts," he says, tilting his head with concern.

Lost in my own thoughts, is he kidding me? The only thought I have right now is him clearing my desk and fucking me right here and right now. *Oh, Samantha, get it together. Remember Shelby's words, you can't sleep with every interviewee or you will never have enough employees to open the place.* For the love of God, I pray this guy is gay. If he's not, I will have to say screw Shelby and her sensible advice. What she doesn't know won't hurt her. In no way, shape, or form can I pass up a piece of ass this good-looking.

"Really, it's okay. I can come back if this is a bad time for you?"

"Nonsense." I wave him off. "I'm sorry, I feel as if I'm having déjà vu. Have we met before? Maybe in the ladies room at Cat's Meow in the last stall?" I say with a giggle, standing from my desk and extending my hand to him. He gives me a nice firm shake with a big smile ignoring my comment for the moment. I walk around him to shut and lock the door. The sound of the lock turning appears to make him uncomfortable. Before walking back to where he stands, I quickly undo one button of my blouse while his back is to me. Instead of sitting back behind my desk, I sit on the desk directly in front of him with my arms crossed helping my cleavage along. Stretching my long toned legs out, I cross my ankles giving him a nice view of my thighs peeking out from my short grey skirt.

"No, ma'am, I don't believe we have ever met before," he says with a blush crossing his cheeks.

"Please do not call me ma'am or Ms. Champagne. It's Samantha; call me Samantha. I'm sorry, I was daydreaming when you came in, what did you say your name was?"

"Parke, Parke Matherne."

"Okay, Parke, tell me why a stud like you wants to work in a strip club as a bartender? You do know this is a female strip club, right?" I say, looking him up and down with no apologies.

His eyes shift to the short hem of my skirt then back to my face. "I'm in college right now and the part-time night gig is perfect for my schedule. And yes, I know this is a female strip club. I have no interest in stripping myself."

"That is a pity. I would pay good money to see that. No offense, but what in the hell are you still doing in college at—" I look down at his résumé to find his age because I know he's over twenty-five. "You're thirty-two? I mean, you look damn good for thirty-two, but shouldn't you be married to a supermodel with three perfect kids running around, or something like that?"

"No offense taken, but I'm not ready to be strapped down with a wife and kids. I have been in the military since I graduated high school and decided after a few tours in the Middle East that I wanted to do something different."

"Well, do you have any experience tending bar?"

"Not much, but I catch on fast. I can do both bartending and security details if needed."

"I need something secured alright." Leaning over to him, I put my hands on the arms of his chair boxing him in. His gaze is powerful; I can feel his want for me and his smell is heady and overwhelming. I look into his black eyes. "What ya say you forget about this job? You see, I have this no sleeping with my employees rule, and I really want you to take me right here on this desk. Don't you want to take me right here on this desk, Parke?" I ask, running my finger down his jaw line watching it flinch as I go.

His gaze is intense with no change in emotions. All signs of a shy schoolboy have been wiped away by a more confident stare. He leans in closer to me. We're now nose to nose and I can feel his warm minty breath on my face. "While that's a very tempting offer, I will have to pass."

"Are you gay?" I counter. "I can usually pick the gay ones out, but you didn't strike me as gay." I shift my gaze directly down to his lap to find his erection bulging. Oh man, it looks so freaking big and delicious. "If you're not gay, what's the problem?" I say with a smirk and look down into his lap. "Your lips are telling me no, but your cock is jumping at the chance."

He doesn't flinch, falter, or move. "Ms. Champagne, you're correct. I would love to fuck you right here on that desk, but you see, as a thirteen-year Army man, I'm a rule follower. And clearly, you stated you have a no screwing your employees rule; therefore, I can do without. I need this job more than I need a fast fuck on your desk, no disrespect. You see, most bars around here are owned by men who don't share your rule. They fuck all their employees, and they don't want a man like me as their competition so they don't hire me. I have one year of school left; hire me for one year, and I promise to fuck you so hard on this desk as a going away gift you will beg me to stay." A grin now spread across his face. I watch his pink wet tongue dart out and over his lips.

I stand in disgust from the sour taste of rejection. I have interviewed eight men for this job; five did me on this very desk without hesitation. Two were gay so they got the job, and Shelby recommended Jackson to me so I couldn't even entertain the thought of sleeping with him since she would have killed me. But this is the only one I can really say I wanted. There's something about him, something mysterious. I'm not sure I can hire him and contain myself around him.

I turn and walk behind my desk sitting back into my large leather chair with a smile on my face trying not to allow the rejection to show.

"Mr. Matherne, please leave your contact information with my assistant, and we will give you a call if we can use your services."

"Thank you, I hope to hear from you soon," he says as he turns and walks right out of my door and my life!

"OMG, who's the hunk that just left?" Shelby asks, entering my office while I'm still deep in thought about how to process the rejection.

I just stare up at her at a loss for words. I still can't

believe he just told me NO.

"Tell me you didn't," she scolds, "I thought we agreed you would stop screwing your potential employees?"

"I wish I could say I did, but I didn't." I look up at her in shock.

"You seriously expect me to believe that? You both look flushed."

"He fucking told me no, Shelby! Can you believe that shit? No, he told me no."

She looks just as surprised as I feel. "Are you kidding me? Did he really?"

"Do I look like I'm fucking kidding you? I have never been so humiliated in all my life."

"Did he say why? He didn't look gay, but you can't always tell by looking at someone these days."

"Yeah, he told me why. He said he wanted the job too much. I had opened my big mouth about my number one rule, no sleeping with employees and that was it."

"Oh, I love this guy, you need to hire him right away. You will never meet someone like this again. It means he values his job, the rules, and he wants to work."

"I don't know. I'm not sure I can work with him now. I made a complete ass of myself." I put my head in my hands and hide my face in utter shame.

"Oh, honey, don't worry about that. When you hire him, apologize and blame your behavior on the stress of losing your husband."

"Ugh, why can't I just get it together like you?"

"You will. Stop trying so hard and let it happen naturally. Forget about the sex and become friends. See where it leads."

"Do I look like I want a friend? You're my friend. I have enough friends. I don't need any more friends; my circle of friends is closed," I yell.

"Let it happen; try it for me. Stop trying to kill your pain with mindless sex."

"Okay, okay, enough depressing shit. What brought you to the city today?"

In typical Shelby style, she doesn't hesitate, getting right to the point. "I have been volunteering at the battered woman's shelter once a month, and today I met a young woman that would work well here. You told me you still needed a few more dancers, right?"

"Yeah, but I don't need a crazy man coming here to start trouble. What's her deal?"

"Her name is Sunny, and she's not from around here. She's not even from Louisiana so her crazy man shouldn't be an issue; he has no idea where she is. The shelter asks all volunteers not to ask about their personal situation, but Sunny opened up to me. She was a stripper in the past until her boyfriend made her quit to become a waitress. Long story short, she doesn't really want to strip, but if she could be one of your show girls, that would be great!"

"Shelby, Shelby, Shelby," I say, shaking my head. She has no clue how this stuff works. This girl really does live under a rock. "While I'm trying to sell this place off as a high-class Burlesque show, it's still a strip club. All my girls will rotate from the stripper stage, as barely dressed show girls in the club room, and all will do equal time in the hanging bird cage in the sex room." I say this with a stern look letting her know this is not an option. But she still doesn't get it.

"Come on, can't you make one exception? You do own the place, you know?"

"Hell no! Sorry, Shelby, I can't do that, it's all or nothing. If she wants to come by and see the place, she will understand this is not the typical trashy strip club she has worked at in the past. You have to understand, for the money I pay my girls, they have to do it all. And they have to be absolutely stunning, model-like beautiful. What does she look like?"

"Well, she's a little banged up right now with an awful

dye job, but even with all that, she is stunning. She has these emerald eyes that are like nothing you have ever seen."

"Tell her to come by tomorrow at 11:00 a.m. and I will see what I can do. But I won't promise you I will hire her."

"That's a deal, thanks. So when is the grand opening?"

As I tell her Thanksgiving night, she looks at me with a sour face crinkling her nose. Rock, I tell you, she lives under a rock.

"Why would you have a grand opening on a Thursday, and a holiday for that matter?"

"Because that's one of the biggest club nights in the business."

Her eyes grow wide as if she has learned something new. "Wow, I had no idea."

With a shake of my head and a laugh, I say, "Imagine that."

"You are mean, do you know that?" she says, laughing back at me.

I hesitate to ask, but I really would love to have her here on the Grand Opening. I'm not sure they will come after their sex room experience, but I ask anyway. "So you and Grant are coming, right?"

She shifts in her chair, looking down at the floor. "Come on, don't wuss out on me. I need you here. This is a big deal for me."

She looks up at me with kind eyes. She knows how much her friendship means to me. She was there for me when Phillip died like no other friend could have been.

"I will try my best to get the kids taken care of and see if Grant will go for it. You know he's not hot about you having the sex room."

"I know, but you two can stay on the club level. This club is different from Savannah's Closet. Our main goal is not a sex club, it's to have options. Come on, let me show you the VIP section we just finished putting together. I have a section for just the basketball crew."

"I have to say I'm not sure Sunny will be ready in three weeks. I mean, her face is pretty bad. You know women don't go to the shelter for shits and giggles. Her face is still a little swollen, her bruises are pretty dark, and she has a nasty cut on her lip."

"Can the girl dance or not? Let her know the bruises are not a concern of mine. I have an ultimate set of tools called Carmella. She is the best makeup artist in New Orleans. I have a feeling I may not be able to keep her much longer; once the movie crews get wind of her talent, she will be gone with the wind. I intend on paying her nicely to urge her to stay, but I'm not sure I will be able to keep up with the Hollywood money that comes in when they're filming in area. Make Sunny aware of the fact that this is a high-class establishment and that's what I expect from my dancers and that is what I pay for."

I pull Shelby by the arm and walk her down to the club level so she can see that it's just a regular club on that floor.

"Wow, this is really chic. The red, black, and white color scheme is classic yet contemporary." She turns to me, grasping my shoulders as she bounces up and down with excitement. "We really can hang out in this roped-off section and have our own little party? I will feel like a Kardashian, this is so cool."

"So you think you can talk Grant into coming with you?"

"Yes, after seeing it for myself, I think I can manage it. I may be forced to hire a limo. He won't say no to that." We laugh, as we both know what will go on in the limo. Shelby and Grant have come a long way since their "Cyber Incident," and I'm glad to see she's trying to break out of her shell.

CHAPTER 2

Sunny – Formerly known as Mary

I stand in the front of an old brick building, frozen in place. I feel a wave of terror wash over me as I realize I can't do this. This is what put me in the very position I'm in today. Stripping in that hellhole is where I met Rex, where two years of bliss turned into a year of torture.

My mind flashes back to the good times with Rex, when he treasured me and cared about me—cared about my opinion, my dreams, and my future. Rex was so caring in the first two years. When my grandmother died, he had his motorcycle club The Flaming Dragons pay to bury her, and then he gave me a place to stay.

I stand out on the cobblestone street in a trance, tugging on the heart locket around my neck. This is the only thing I have left of my old life. It was my grandmother's locket. Rex had it cleaned and repaired so she would be with me forever after she died. I have worn it every day since then. It's the only thing I took when I escaped him and the club.

Moving in with him and quitting the strip club was the biggest mistake of my life. I had nothing of my own, and working at the coffee shop barely afforded me enough money to buy decent clothes. I was trapped. Rex became the president of The Flaming Dragons and he changed. I will never forget the first day he hit me. I was so in love with him, and I never saw it coming. I didn't grow up in an MC life; I had no clue what an old lady was much less what she was supposed to do and not do. We had been together for about a year, but I never went to the clubhouse or hung around with the other guys. Once I moved in with him, I was officially his old lady and was expected to show my face at the club. However, no one filled me in on the rules.

Nine months later

We are hanging out at a pig roast, and I question him about a run they are getting ready to make. He gives me a death stare and says, "Shut the fuck up, Mary, it's none of your business." He says it in front of all his brothers. I am pissed; he has never acted this way toward me before so I am shocked. I don't respond to him at the moment and simply walk away as the anger is too intense for me to process. Once we get home, he blows up at me shouting and screaming about club rules and old lady stuff that makes no sense to me.

"What in the hell has gotten into you, Rex? I don't know the first thing about being an old lady. I had no idea I couldn't be myself. You didn't have to be an asshole about it. I simply asked you where you were going and what you were doing."

His eyes fill with so much rage it terrorizes me. He stalks toward me with determination. "I told you, I'm the president and no one questions me, no one! Especially my old lady. Did you forget the conversation we had before we went to the roast?"

He now stands directly in front of me and I can almost see the steam coming from his ears. I don't know what came over me but the fear dissipates and my anger takes over. "No, I didn't forget. But you need to remember I'm not one of you brothers. I didn't sign up for your little club." And that does it. SMACK. I just hear the sound as the pain radiates across my face. I stumble back and fall onto the sofa, covering my face in defense. I feel blood running out of my nose as I sit looking up at him in shock and horror.

"You are my old lady, you are my property, property of the club. You became my property for life the day you got the club logo tattooed on your back."

That statement enrages me. "I didn't give you

permission to put that tattoo on me," I yell up at him. "In case you forgot, I was completely knocked out when your buddy branded me with your tattoo."

"You know you wanted that tattoo, but you chickened out at the last minute so we took matters into our own hands. Doesn't matter, you're mine for life. You are the old lady of the president of The Flaming Dragons. I'm telling you now, don't ever question me about club business not here and especially not at the club in front of my brothers. Do you understand me?"

As I shake my head in confirmation, I realize he must have knocked the sense right out of me because I keep at him. "Oh, I understand you alright. You don't want me to question the illegal shit you all have been doing. I don't like it and I don't want to be a part of it."

"Too bad you're in for life," he says with an evil smirk. How could I have fallen for him? He looks like the devil looking down at me as he towers over me with power.

"I'm not in for life, I didn't marry you. I can leave whenever I want." What in the hell is wrong with me? I know I should shut the hell up while he is acting this way, but I can't help myself. I think he has to come back to me. I have to be able to bring him back to the way he was; this is not him.

He grabs me by my arm pulling me up off the sofa and pushing me up against the wall hard. He rips my sundress down the middle by the seam. "Mary, in our world, this tattoo right here," he says, pushing his finger deep into my back over the ugly tattoo of a dragon spitting flames from its mouth with his name tattooed within the flames. "Turn your face to me, look at it," he yells. I ignore him with my face still pressed against the wall and my eyes shut.

"No, I didn't agree to that tattoo."

He squeezes my face with his fingers turning it to him. "No, you didn't, but it's there. You're mine and I'm going to mold you to be the old lady of a president. You understand me?"

At that point, I know he will hit me again if I don't agree so I shake my head yes. The next day, I pack my clothes, and with the little money I had, I get on a bus and head anywhere but here. I take the first bus out of St. Louis. I have no family to run to. My mom died of cancer when I was little and I never knew my dad. My grandmother raised me and now she's gone. I have no one left but myself. The bus I jumped on is headed to Chicago. I hope the city is big enough to hide me from the other Flaming Dragons. My breath catches and my heart starts pounding when I realize they have a chapter in Chicago. Damn it, I should have headed south; there are no clubs south of the Mason Dixon line.

After four hours on this hot and smelly bus, it stops in a small town right outside of Chicago. The bus driver stands up to announce the bus is having some mechanical issues and we will be stuck in this town for four additional hours while we wait for a new bus to arrive. I have a knot in the pit of my stomach and can't shake the feeling that something bad is going to happen; I just know it, but what? I try to steer clear of the creepy guy from the bus but the feeling increases. Two hours into our wait, the other shoe drops. I hear the roar of Harleys.

It's them. I know it in my heart. How in the hell did they find me here? Maybe it's a coincidence? I turn and hurry into the gas station hoping they will ride by. But they don't! I hear the engines stop right in front of the store. I see a group of them enter the store and that's when I see The Flaming Dragons patch. My heart free falls into my stomach, and I know they are here for me. My feet are frozen; I have to get out of here. They are covering the exit, so I make a dash for the bathroom hoping there's a back exit. I make the turn and see a Harley just outside the door through the dirty window. *Damn it!* I make a turn and rush into the women's bathroom hoping they won't come in due to the number of people around.

I am so wrong. I rush into a stall, lock the door, and put my feet up on the toilet when I hear the entry door fly open.

"Mary, I know you're in here. Don't you know you can't hide from me?" I hear Rex's voice. "We are only going to discuss this one time, woman. You are mine for life. Now if you want your life to end today, it will be here with me, but you will be with me when you take your last breath. Don't you know how much I need you? You love me, Mary, I'm the only family you have," he roars over the stall door.

I hear the bikes right outside the window. They have all moved from the front of the store to the back. How can I have been so stupid? Running to the back of the store means no one will even know I'm gone. With one powerful kick, the stall door is smashed open. Terror fills my chest and I can't breathe. I can't move, not even to look up at him.

"I will give you this one time. That's it, just this one time considering you really didn't know the rules, woman. I know I must have scared you when I hit you but know I don't want to put my hands on you again. So please don't make me. Just do as I say and don't ask questions, and this will all work out. Okay, Mary, you get me?"

His tone is so matter of fact like I'm a possession and not person as if I have no feelings. I know I am trapped, no way out. His reach is too far for me. I have no place to run and no one to protect me. I sit crouched on the dirty toilet seat frozen in place and trembling. He takes one step to me and wipes the streaming tears from my face with his thumb. I shiver in disgust as he lifts my face to look at him.

"Don't ever run from me again, Mary. I will find you no matter where you go. Do you understand that you are mine? Everything you own is mine and can be tracked by me. Now let's go."

He picks me up and I'm scared to death—scared to go with him and scared to fight. I can't live the rest of my life with a man who thinks nothing of hitting me and treating me like an object. Boy was I stupid. Why couldn't I see that getting involved with a member of an MC was bad news? I decide to let him take me because let's face it, I have no other choice really. I will have to gain his trust before I can come up with a better plan to run.

CHAPTER 3

Sunny – Formerly known as Mary

I spend the next few weeks trying to act normal, as if nothing happened. I regain his trust enough for him to allow me to go back to work at the coffee shop. One day while washing clothes, I hear something hit the tile floor with a light clink. It sounds like change or maybe even an earring, so I bend down to find it. All the blood drains from my face when I see it. I had heard Tec talking about his new device they are using to track shipments. The scene replays in my mind crystal clear. "Dude, these things are groundbreaking in the computer world," Tec told Rex as he held the little device between his fingertips. "They can get wet, withstand heat, and can be tracked across the globe. The only thing needed is a cell tower to pick up the signal."

I recall that day like yesterday back when I was still trying to figure out what their shipments were. I now hold the same tiny object in my hand that Tec held up to Rex that day. I quickly pull the rest of the clothes from the washer trying to figure out where it came from. Maybe Rex had it in his pocket and forgot about it. "Holy shit! That son of a bitch," I scream, throwing each piece of clothing out piece-by-piece only to discover it's all my clothes in this batch. I pick up one piece to feel it carefully along all the seams. "Damn, it's sewed right in the seam." I go through each piece of clothing on the floor and find one shirt without a tracker and realize this is the one it fell from. I get up and run to my closet checking the rest of my clothes, and sure enough, everything I own, down to my panties and bra, has a tiny tracker placed in each and every piece.

My knees give out and I hit the floor sobbing, "How am I going to get out of this hellhole called my life? He knows every freaking move I make." I'm confident my movements are monitored on his cell phone if I know him.

He told me that day in the gas station that everything I owned could be tracked by him. It just didn't register with me that he actually meant I am being TRACKED like a fucking animal. Feeling absolutely helpless, I bow my head into my hands and do the only thing I have left to do, pray. "God, please help me, I don't deserve this. Please send me someone to help me get away from him. He will kill me soon."

After a few moments of sobbing, I realize Rex will be home soon and I can't let him know I know. Things have not been going well with the club and he has been in awful moods. From what I've heard by eavesdropping, the FBI is hot on their tail. I need to get out and soon. I shake it off and start picking up the clothes. I tell myself, "Suck it up girl get your shit together." On my way out the door headed to work early in efforts to miss seeing Rex, I physically run into his hard, drunk body on the way out the door.

"Where you running off to in such a hurry?" he slurs.

"Work," I say, quickly trying to brush past him.

He grabs me roughly by the arm. "It's only five o'clock, your shift don't start till seven, what's the fucking hurry?"

"I thought I would help Cindy with the evening rush. Katy called in sick."

"What about helping me out?" he says as he kisses down my neck. My stomach rolls from the smell of whiskey and cigarettes. I know he wants sex, and I'm tired of giving in to him."

"I have to go, Rex, I will make it up to you when I get back, promise," I say with the best fake smile I can muster. I try to walk away without making him angry. No such luck. His strong hands slam me up against the door so hard the doorknob puts a hole in the sheetrock. I hear a loud crack as my ribs collide with the door knocking the wind out of me.

"Woman, I'm tired of your excuses. I only need five minutes if that much," he grunts as he licks my neck.

I know I can't fight him. I need to do what needs to be done in order to get out of here alive. And being in this house does not help me. His tongue slides from my ear, back down my neck, and over the top of my breasts. His hands are rough as he pulls the snap buttons of my uniform top open. He then pulls my bra down giving himself access to my nipples. His body has me pinned to the wall. As he sucks my nipple, I feel his hand under my skirt pulling my panties to the side. He looks up into my eyes. "Why do you look at me with so much hate, Mary? I took care of you when you had no one. I have not laid a hand on you since the day you ran from me. What else do you want from me?"

I have no words for him. My face says it all and I can't hide it. My disgust for him is too deep and there's no turning the clock back. He leans down to my ear whispering, "You know, the girls at the club beg me to fuck them twice? I shouldn't have to beg my old lady for one piece of ass." He chuckles.

I don't know why his admission of infidelity enrages me, but it does. I haven't wanted to sleep with him but have a few times since my runaway incident. I try to make it seem normal but I feel betrayed. It is a reflex, not a thought, when my hand goes across his face with a smack so loud I immediately know I am in trouble.

I almost lose consciousness when his hand comes back across mine. He catches me before I hit the floor to berate me, "You fucking bitch, don't you know I only want you? I want you to want me but you don't so I'm forced to fuck the skanks at the club. You look at me as if I'm a piece of shit and I'm sick of it."

I hear his belt buckle come undone and fear spreads like wildfire throughout my entire body. Is he going to beat me or fuck me? I'm not sure which is worse at the moment. But I'm still too dazed from his hit to process that he has pulled me to the floor. It takes me a few seconds to realize he has entered me and is pushing in and out with angry grunts. I feel him hit me again in the face, and my mind checks out when I feel blood drip from the corner of my mouth. He can have my body, but my soul is mine and I won't give it to him. Moments later, I feel his weight lift off me as a shirt hits me in the face.

"Here, clean yourself up and get your ass to work, I'm done with you." The sound of his heavy boots walking away, followed by the door slamming, is pure heaven. I sigh in relief hearing his bike roar to life spitting up gravel as he takes off down the drive.

Thank God, he's gone. I try to sit up and realize how rough he was. *Did I check out or was I knocked out?* I have deep bruises already starting to appear on my arms, my ribs are killing me, and the shooting pain in the back of my head is almost unbearable. I finally get up enough strength to get off the floor and go to the bathroom to wash out my bloody mouth. I look in the mirror in horror to find my eye almost swollen shut, my lip split, and a developing bruise is starting to take over half of my face.

I can't even cry! My life is so pathetic. I have no hope. If I stay, he will kill me, and if I leave, he will find me and kill me. I see the evil in his eyes; it's only a matter of time if I stay.

I take a deep breath and do my best to cover the bruises with makeup using my trembling hands. I literally drag myself into the coffee shop. I have no idea how I will make it through a shift, but I would rather be here than home with Rex.

CHAPTER 4

Sunny – Formerly known as Mary

I open the door to the coffee shop and Cindy rushes over to me. "What did that bastard do to you, Mary? Are you okay, do you need to go to the hospital, honey?" She tries to put her hand up to my face but I push it away.

"I'm fine, I will be fine. It was my fault. I should have kept my mouth shut." I slap at her hands again to stop her from making a fuss and walk to the back to get my apron. I hear her footsteps and roll my eyes. I turn to her trying not to lose it. "Look, Cindy, I know you mean well, but please I don't want to hear it. I don't stay with him because I love him. I stay because he will kill me if I leave." I shrug past her out into the shop to take my place behind the counter. I see Joe watching me closely. He is such a nice man. He's old enough to be my father. I do my best to crack a smile at him, "You want the usual, Joe?"

He shakes his head with a kind smile. "Yep, you know me, same old, same old."

I bring him his coffee black like he likes it. When I sit the mug down in front of him, he gently places his hand on top of mine. "Mary, I don't want to offend you, but you need help." I pull my hand away defensively.

"Thanks for the concern but really I'm fine," I say, starting to turn away from him.

"No, you're not. Please give me five minutes and let me tell you how I can help you."

He wants to help me? How does he think he can help me? "Two minutes is all I have. I have had a rough day and I need to serve the other customers."

"I know more than you think. I know who you run with and I know you're being watched."

My eyes grow wide as I'm surprised by his comments.

He's not a biker. He's a riverboat pilot. How in the hell would he know who I run with? I lean in closer to him not wanting the rest of the customers to hear us. "What do you think you know?"

He whispers back to me, "I know you are the old lady of the president of The Flaming Dragons. And I know you tried to leave him a while ago and he went after you at that gas station right outside of Chicago. I also know he is fed up with what he calls your attitude and he's openly screwing anyone that will have him at the club."

I stare at him with my mouth gaping wide in surprise. How could this man know this? He is one of my regular customers who typically engages me in conversation, but I have never given him private details. "How do you know that?" I ask not sure I really want to know the answer to that.

"I have friends that are members of The Flaming Dragons and they talk. Usually they don't, but apparently they are not happy with their current president. They don't like the way he treats his old lady," he says, nodding his head to my growing bruises. "His brothers don't condone hitting women. But when I hear them talk, they talk about their sorrow for you because they know there's no way out for you. And due to the code of the club, they can't go against the president to help you."

I start to tremble again knowing he's right and reality hits me hard. A single tear slips down my face, and I swipe it away quickly.

"I know this is hard to hear, but you have to plaster a smile on that pretty face of yours and act naturally," he says, looking at me calmly as if we were chatting about the weather.

"Listen, we only have a few minutes to get this done. The Dragons tapped into the surveillance feed here and the surrounding areas are covered as well. But I know where the dead spaces are, and I can get you out of—"

I stop him short with a smile on my face, but my tone is helpless and defeated. "How in hell do you think you can do that?" I ask, pressing my skirt down to make it appear as if everything is normal. I inform him that every stitch of clothing I own is tracked down to my fucking panties.

"I know," he says, looking down at his coffee, "That's how they found you the last time you ran. Just listen very carefully and I can help you. Please let me help you, Mary," he pleads and waits for me to agree.

I shake my head in confirmation.

He smiles. "I'm going to pay you in a minute for my coffee, and with my cash, I have instructions folded in between the bills. Go to the bathroom for a break and follow the directions VERY carefully and quickly," he stresses. "I promise to get you out of here and somewhere safe."

I look down the counter to see a customer has come in and sat down two stools away from us. I put a finger up to Joe letting him know I will be right back. I'm not sure I can process this. Should I really just take off with him? What if it's a set up? But I have known Joe for a year and he has been nothing but nice. I take my new customer's order and pour him some coffee. Thank goodness, he's a white-collar worker and not a friend of The Flaming Dragons. I walk back over to Joe and decide I have to make a move. I will die if I stay, so I may as well go down in flames trying to get the hell out of here.

When I approach Joe, he leans in toward me. "Time is running out, Mary. I lost my daughter to a man like Rex. I don't want to watch him kill you like that piece of shit killed my baby girl. You in?"

I shake my head yes. He stands up to pull a wad of cash out of his pocket sifting though it to give me what I need. He walks out the door and to his truck. I stand there for a moment trying to regain my composure. I reach my hand out to collect his money and then turn my back to the surveillance camera. I put the money inside the register and slip what appears to be the tip in my pocket. Just as I do, the door swings opens and Janie walks in for her shift.

She yells from the door with two customers in the shop, "What the hell? That motherfucker put his hands on you again?"

I look down in utter embarrassment. It's bad enough you can see it, but do we really have to announce it to the world? I motion to her with my fingers over my lips to keep it down. When she finally reaches me, I pull her close. "Janie, come on, you know I'm stuck. But now that you're here, can you take over for a few minutes so I can regroup? I think it's time for some touch-up makeup in the mirror." I give her a weak pleading smile.

"Of course, hon, but the only thing that is going to fix your face is a bullet to Rex's brain," she says with anger in her eyes. I really think she would do it if she owned a gun. My body shakes at the thought of guns. I hate them. They make me very nervous.

I give her another gentle smile wishing it were that simple. I rush to the bathroom stall to read Joe's note. The paper appears to be a bit old. Judging it by the creases, I'm sure he has had this in his wallet for some time waiting for the right moment to help me. I look up. *Thank you, God, for answering my prayers and sending Joe to help me.* I know this is a sign and I just have to go with it. I instantly feel a wave of calm and determination. This is my only way out; I will do whatever his paper tells me to do.

1. Unplug the cameras on your way out of the bathroom.
2. Go to the backside of the coffee shop, and pick up the brown bag.
3. Take EVERYTHING OFF! Put the clothes on from the bag and put your

clothes into it. Leave your coat in the stall.

4. Walk out the back door with the bag without speaking to anyone. Go two blocks toward the river, keeping on the far right side of the street to avoid video feed.

I will be there waiting for you.

I follow his instructions precisely. I'm amazed at how calm I am as I walk down the street toward the river. I see Joe's red truck in a distance. I pick up my pace and hop in as my heart starts to beat in my throat. So much for the calm feeling.

"Thanks Joe—" I start, but he cuts me off.

"No time for talk. Now let's get the hell out of here," he says, pulling off quickly.

"Where we going?" I ask nervously.

"We are going down the Mississippi River to New Orleans. You do know I'm a river boat pilot, right?" he asks, shifting his eyes to me momentarily.

"Yeah, I do, but how will that work?" I ask nervously. We are not to the boat yet, and my nerves are starting to come undone quickly.

"You are going to get on my ship under the radar, and we're going to sail down the river to New Orleans, and I'm going to take you to the Battered Women's shelter where they can help you. They will house you, counsel you, help you get a new identity, and train you for a job."

"Really, they will give me a new identity?"

"Yes, I tried to get my Lilly to go but she refused. He killed her two days after I begged her to go to the shelter." His face reddens and his eyes fill with tears he tries to hold back.

"Oh, Joe, I'm so sorry to hear that." I reach over and

squeeze his hand offering whatever comfort I can.

"That's why I couldn't sit by and listen to what The Dragons were saying and not help you. That's when I started to make the coffee shop my daily hangout. I wanted to watch over you, get to know you, and gain your trust. I made a plan and hoped it would work when needed."

I start to cry out of happiness. It warms my heart to know that a total stranger cared enough about me to do all this. I give his hand a harder squeeze. "Thank you, Joe, thank you," I say, looking at him through my tears of hope.

I look up and we are now entering what appears to be the shipyard. Stopping near the train tracks, Joe shouts over the noise of the passing trains, "Hand me your bag of clothes and wait here. Lock the door and don't get out for anything, you hear me?" I shake my head in confirmation.

He gets out and I watch him toss each piece of my clothing onto different train cars. All the trains are on different tracks. There are tons of trains lined up waiting and some are already starting to move out. He runs back to the truck, and I unlock the door letting him in and we are off again.

He says with a chuckle, "You will be scattered all over the country in a few hours. By the time they realize you're gone, they will have no clue in what direction you went."

"Freaking genius, do you know that? That is genius," I say with a huge smile. *This may really work.*

We park and sit in the parking lot while Joe makes a phone call. "Jimmy, its 4:45, what the hell are you doing? Yeah, well, I need you to start the meals. I'm freaking starving. I know you usually man the entrance, but I'm pulling up now, getting my shit out of the truck, and it's just you and me on this run. I will lock the gate behind me. Yeah, thanks," he says into the phone and hangs up. We watch from the truck as Jimmy walks off the deck and into the cabin out of our sight. We start to walk to the ship and stop at the loading area. He turns to me. "You stay behind me and walk as quickly as you can. I will get you to a safe place."

"Okay," I say as my heart picks up a beat again. If it beats any faster, I may go into cardiac arrest. I feel safe with Joe, but I still have my ears out for the unmistakable sound of Harleys.

We board the ship safely without anyone knowing, no bikes, no Rex, just us. Joe shows me to my cabin and gets me settled. He gives me some meds for the pain and shows me that I have a bathroom in the small cabin, a bed, and a small table with a chair.

"You will be safe here. Please rest. You need it. I will bring you food in a little bit. There is a phone here, but only use it if it's an emergency. Just pick it up and dial zero. When I answer, hang up. I will know it's you and I will come to you. But I doubt you will need to use it."

The trip takes about three days, I think? I was in and out on pain pills Joe gave me, which I normally don't take, but my head and ribs were killing me. The rest was welcomed. I can't remember the last time I was able to sleep so soundly.

We finally reach New Orleans and it's a relief to be so far away from Rex. Joe must have known The Flaming Dragons don't have a chapter here so it's the perfect place. I sneak off the boat while Joe causes a distraction and meet him in the parking lot. He had rented a car and had it ready to drive me to the shelter.

We pull up in front of an old warehouse building on a cobblestone street. The feeling I have for Joe is overwhelming. What a gift he is; he put his life on the line for me. Without him, Rex would have killed me without a doubt.

But sadness rushes over me thinking about Joe's safety. If The Dragons find out it was him, they will kill him for sure. I reach over the seat while we still sit parked and give Joe the tightest hug I can with what I'm sure is broken ribs. Tears start to stream down my face. "Thank you so much for saving me, Joe. I don't have a dad to look out for me. Without you, I would have wound up dead, and soon."

He smiles at me. "It's the least I could do."

I return with worry, "Are they going to know it was you, Joe? If they find out it was you—"

He cuts me off, patting me on the back, "Shhh, Mary, they will have no way of knowing. I never told a soul of my plans. I just kept open ears and never asked any questions about you. It's all good."

We get out of the car and stand at the front door. I turn to embrace him again. As he hugs me back with such love, I feel his loss. I feel him heaving, trying not to breakdown. He pulls back and looks at me with eyes filled with tears.

"Glad I could help you, Mary. From the day I met you, I knew you were my ray of sunshine. Thank you for bringing me out of the darkness. I can never bring my Lilly back, but saving you helps me feel like I have done something for her. You have many sunny days ahead of you.

I stretch up on my tiptoes and give Joe a gentle kiss on his cheek. "Thank you, I will never be able to say that enough."

He motions to me with his hands swatting in the air. "That's enough. I'm glad I could help. Now let's get you settled."

He opens the door to the shelter and to my new life. Ms. Annabelle is the shelter director, and she takes care of everything for me. She shows me around the sleeping quarters, which is a long room with several bunk beds lined up on both sides of the walls with one there waiting for me. She looks at me with care and concern.

"I know it's not much," she says, looking around the room, "but it's safe. That's the most important thing for you right now is to know you're safe. Now let's go to the office and get all the paperwork straight." I follow her to the office where my life changes forever.

Ms. Annabelle had the power due to my situation to give me an entirely new identity. She lets me choose my name, and I could not help but think of Joe and pick Sunny. I want to turn a new leaf and always look at the bright side so Sunny it is. We spent the rest of that day going to the DMV with my new birth certificate, getting a new license, going over the rules, starting counseling, and learning about my new hometown of New Orleans.

The other women in the shelter were very nice and forthcoming. I could not believe their stories were so similar to mine. I have sat up at night thinking I'm the only person in the world that is weak enough to put up with this. I beat myself up mentally for so long and it wasn't my fault. This is going to be good for me, but I'm not sure how long I can stay in this place. It's very cramped with no privacy. I need to find a job and fast.

CHAPTER 5

Sunny - *Present day*

My heart warms as I remember the events of the last few days. I shake my head in efforts to bring myself out of my daydream. The sound of a jazz band coming up the street pulls me out of the past. I look down at the watch Ms. Annabelle gave me to help keep me on time and realize I have been standing here daydreaming for the last twenty minutes.

What in the hell am I doing here? Working in a strip club put me in the position I'm in today. I would have never been introduced to the likes of anyone in an MC had I not worked there. I turned to run as far and as fast as I could in the opposite direction. With one swift movement away from the club, I hit a brick wall, a wall of muscle. The force knocks me off my feet but I don't hit the ground. I hear a voice that belongs to the man now holding me in his arms.

"Sorry, ma'am, I was coming out to make sure you were okay?"

His hands hold tightly around my waist and over my bruised ribs. I squirm in pain as he lets go noticing my wincing.

"Did I hurt you? I'm sorry, I had no idea you were bolting," he says, trying to smooth things over. He looks kind of scary in a sexy uncover cop way.

"No, you didn't hurt me. I'm fine," I say while smoothing my clothes back into place.

"You are clearly not fine, you seem to be in a lot of pain."

"I am hurt, but you didn't cause it. I had a bit of an accident last week and I have bruised ribs. I'll be fine. Thanks for catching me but I have to run." I try to turn and walk away. He gives me a knowing glance as he gently puts his hand on my arm, which makes me freeze in fear. What is he going to do, who is this man? Looking up at him, I know he could really hurt me if he wanted. He is a large man appearing to be a few inches over six foot with the most amazing, sexy, muscular build which tells me he works out daily. He has a short military haircut that exposes his defined jawline. His face is so perfect and squared it appears to have been chiseled from stone. He is perfect in every way if you were going to mold a man, strong cheekbones, defined brows, and the most piercing blue eyes I have ever seen. He seems safe but not welcoming.

He puts his hands up to assure me he didn't mean to scare me. I blush in horror that I'm so messed up and scared of everything. I hate Rex and all he has done to me. The perfect male specimen puts his hand out to me introducing himself. "I'm Jackson and I'm sorry I scared you. Are you Sunny?"

I just stare up at him. I'm still not used to going by that name yet, and I shouldn't trust anyone. "How do you know my name?" I mutter not giving him my hand.

"Samantha said a stunning woman named Sunny was coming by at eleven hundred hours. She mentioned you were a bit hesitant about going back to stripping. I've been watching you stand at the door for the last twenty minutes. When you didn't move, I thought I would come out and make sure you were okay, which was at the exact moment you decided to run."

"Sorry, I don't think I can go in." I blush and look down at my feet on the cobblestone street.

"I understand if you don't want to strip, but if you are going to strip, this is the place to do it."

He is serious because I have never met this man and he thinks he is going to tell me where he thinks I should work. I stiffen in annoyance standing tall, as tall as I can with my 5'5" frame. "Oh yeah? And how many strip clubs have you stripped in?" I don't even know where that tone came from. I almost don't recognize my own voice as it passes my ears. I'm tired of taking shit from people, and I will be Goddamned if this stranger is going to tell me where I should work just because he is gorgeous.

He gives me a small smile breaking from his tough man demeanor, and with a kind voice, he says, "I have never worked as a stripper, but I have worked security in quite a few. All the clubs I have worked for in the past have been dumps with sleaze balls for owners. But not this place, sunshine, this place has a woman for an owner, and she has deep pockets with the intent of making it more than a strip club. She cares about her girls. There's a high cover for the purpose of not letting in the clientele you are accustomed to seeing."

What the heck is he talking about? I have never worked in a club with a cover. Who goes to a high-class strip joint? I look up at him and narrow my eyes. "Really, what type of customers will I see here?" I ask with the same defensive tone.

"You will see businessmen that make six figures or more per hour. Samantha has the club set up as three separate clubs. The cover to the dance club is fifty dollars with another fifty dollars to enter the strip section." His voice changes to a lower note when he says, "Only members are allowed to enter the sex club." Shoving his hands in his pocket, he looks down at me. "There's a hefty annual fee they pay which makes them VIP members and gets them into all the clubs for that flat rate."

I blush a deeper shade of red when he mentions the sex club. Shelby told me about that part but insisted we would only be dancing in it. I push away my anxiety about the sex floor and try to appear unfazed by the mention of it. "Get out of here! What do you mean a dance club?" I ask with a nicer tone, trying to change the subject.

"Come on in," he says, holding his hand out of for me.

"Talk to Samantha. She will give you all the details. Like I said earlier, if you are going to strip, this is the place to do it. You are too beautiful to work at the other nasty joints up the street," he says with a wink.

I look down at my hands when I hear the compliment. It has been awhile since someone has called me beautiful. And just like that, I have fallen under his spell for the moment. "Okay, lead the way." I smile up at his crystal clear blue eyes that dance in his olive-skinned face. I know this is not a pattern I want to start, so I will go straight to the counseling room at the shelter when I get back to work on this.

Samantha

I sit at my desk very annoyed as it's 11:30 and Shelby's girl is a no show. I hear a firm knock at my door and look up to find Jackson standing there with a small woman standing behind him.

"I found your 11:00 lost outside." He gives me a pleading look knowing I'm fuming. I give him a confused look raising my eyebrows up at him. Jackson does not give a shit about anyone. He's tough as nails and only cares about his job. I roll my eyes at him and soften my angry look letting him know I will give her a break. He gives Sunny a wink as he moves from in front of her and stands to the side at the door. *Mental note to self: Question Jackson about that later.* I try to push away my annoyance of her being late and give her a shot.

"Hi, Sunny, my name is Samantha, and Shelby has told me you are looking for a job?" I say, standing and extending my hand to her.

"I'm going to head out if you don't need me," Jackson interrupts, trying to escape my wrath.

"Sure, you go ahead and eat lunch without me, never mind I'm starving," I say jokingly.

"I'm sorry I was late. I can come back another day if you like," Sunny says wearily.

I pat her on the arm and lead her into a chair. "No, honey, I was just messing with the big guy." I tell Jackson to get lost with a shooing motion of my hand.

"I have to be honest with you. I'm not sure I can do this," she says, wringing her hands in her lap very nervously. "I was here on time but frozen in place at the front of the club chasing demons. I can't hide what he has done my face so I might as well tell you. I'm on the run from a guy who did this to me." She points to the obvious bruises on her face and her split lip. "I had a meltdown out there, and your man convinced me to come in," she whispers, finally looking up at me and making eye contact with a small smile.

"Yeah, that's why I keep him around, and he's pretty damn hot. I have to admit, I have this don't sleep with my employees rule that I regret every damn day of my life."

We both chuckle, and I'm glad to see I'm starting to break the ice with her. Before we go any further, there's another knock at the door. "What? Doesn't anyone care that I'm trying to do a freaking interview?" I fuss, yanking open the door. In walks Parke. *Speak of the devil, the number one reason I hate the damn don't sleep with my employees rule.*

"Hey, I'm sorry to interrupt. I just wanted to see if you were almost done and wanted to catch lunch?" he says with a sexy as hell smile.

Did he just ask me to lunch, in front of a possible employee? He hasn't spoken to me about anything other than business the last two weeks he's been employed here.

"Sorry, Parke, I will have to catch you another time. We are just starting here," I say, looking annoyed with him.

"Dinner?" he pleads. That sexy smile he has spreads across his face letting me know he will not leave the room until I agree to eat with him.

"Parke, I'm in the middle of an interview in case you have not noticed." I wave my hand toward Sunny.

"Oh yeah, sorry about that. Hi, my name is obviously Parke, nice to meet you." He extends his hand to Sunny but keeps his attention and eyes trained on me as they shake hands.

"I will get out of your way, Samantha, as soon as you agree to have dinner with me." He crosses his arms and props his lean body against the doorframe like he has all the time in the world.

"Oh geez, you are a pain in the ass, do you know that? Okay, I will go to dinner with you if you leave the room now!" He smiles a devilish grin and walks out the door. Halfway down the hall, he yells, "Nice meeting you, Sunny."

Sunny looks up at me with a humorous grin. "You sure do have a lot of eye candy around here. I can see why you hate that rule."

"I only agreed to go so he would leave us alone. And apparently we need to have a discussion about proper office etiquette during dinner this evening. That will be the topic of discussion," I say with a wink.

Sunny laughs a genuine laugh, which gives me a glimpse of her true beauty. She is stunning. Even with the shiner and a split lit, I can she is truly gorgeous. She has porcelain white skin with broad cheekbones and wide, sexy almond-shaped emerald green eyes. Her hair is long with the right amount of curl without being kinky. It is dyed an awful blonde color, but Carmella can fix that. And her body, it's hard to tell with the baggy clothes she's wearing, but from what I can see, she will work out well.

"So, Sunny, before we discuss anything, let's take a tour of the club so you can get a feel for what type of establishment I'm running here," I say, leading her out of my office.

I'm happy to see Sunny's expression change from guarded to amazed and then excited as we walk around the club. She turns to me when the tour is done.

"This is like nothing I have ever seen in a strip club," she says with an excited voice and wide eyes.

"Because this is more than a strip club. It's a burlesque club. You are not a stripper. You are a performer. If you decide to work here, you will not strip every night."

"Are you kidding me? What would I do on the other nights?" she gasps in surprise.

"Each performer will dance four days a week. Two days in the strip club, one day in the dance club on the boxes, and one day in the sex room.

Sunny's eyes shift to the floor looking away from me at the mention of the sex room. "Is that going to be a problem?" I ask. "Because I can't bend on that. I have to be fair across the board with all my girls," I state with an even, unwavering tone.

"No, that's fine. My only problem is costumes and makeup. I don't have money yet. I came to New Orleans with nothing," she says softly, looking embarrassed.

I see why Shelby gravitated to her. It's so sad to see such a beautiful woman so broken. If I find the guy that did this to her, I may beat the shit out of him myself or at least punch him in the throat one good time. "Don't worry with that. You are not responsible for makeup and costumes just yet. I want a certain look in each room so all costumes will be provided by me. I have also hired a makeup artist that will be on my payroll for the first six months. After that, ya'll are on your own, girlfriend."

With a bright smile, she says, "Where do I sign up?"

"That's what I'm talking about. Be back here tomorrow at 9:00 a.m. to start training and costume fittings. Oh geez, I sure hope you can dance. I suck at this interview stuff. You can dance, right?"

She is now looking at me like I'm nuts. "Yes, I can dance," she says with a giggle.

I show her out and walk back to my office to find Parke sitting at my desk with two Po-boy sandwiches. He looks up at me with a full mouth. "Come eat," he mumbles, as French bread pieces fall from his mouth.

"You brought me lunch?" I ask in surprise.

He swallows and wipes that sexy mouth of his clean to give me his award-winning smile. "Yeah, I couldn't wait 'til dinner, and I figured you must be starving since your interview ran past 12:30. Did you hire her? She was pretty hot."

I try to temper the annoyance I feel when he calls Sunny hot. I'm not sure why it bugged me, but it did. "Yes, I did hire her. And thanks, I'm starving." I pick up the wrapped sandwich sitting next to him. As I unroll it from the white paper, I see it's a plain shrimp sandwich. Looking up at him in confusion, I ask, "How did you know this is what I eat?"

He shrugs his shoulders and replies quickly before taking another bite of his sandwich. "I saw you order it when you took all the employees out for lunch last week."

That was thoughtful of him, especially since I don't even recall what I ordered last week. Ugh, this is getting too nice and mushy for me.

"So tell me, what did you want to discuss because I want to discuss why you think nothing of barging into my office when I have company." I look up at him over my sandwich, taking a bite of the most delicious fried shrimp sandwich ever. I wait for him to finish his bite while I take him in. I typically go for men who are older than myself, never three years younger. I feel pulled to him and I can't quite explain it. Here it goes again, that needy feeling keeps rearing its ugly head and making my heart skip a beat. My thoughts are interrupted by his velvet voice. *Ughhh!*

"Nothing much, we got off on the wrong foot during my interview, and I wanted to start over, as friends and co-workers. Is that okay?"

Friends, co-workers. No, that's not okay. I want to ride him on this desk. He wants to be fucking friends. I should throw my drink at him. Damn you, Samantha, you are the one with the stupid fucking rule.

I try to push away those thoughts and use Shelby's suggested "get out of jail free" card. "Sure, Parke, and I really do apologize for that. I have not been myself since I lost my husband, so please forgive me for my out of character behavior during your interview."

"You're forgiven. And no worries. I know I'm pretty hard to resist," he says with a sly smirk.

"Oh really, you think so?" I ask, almost spitting out my food as I chuckle at him.

"That's what all the ladies tell me anyway. But enough

about me. Tell me more about the club. I feel like I'm missing something here?"

"Yeah, like what?" I say, shifting my head to the side.

"I don't know? I find it odd that members"—he uses his fingers to make quotes—"Well, you know, why would they pay an annual fee of ten thousand dollars just to show up? And to top that off, they have to bring their own sex partner? I don't get that. Is there something else I'm missing?"

I give him a glare that may turn him to dust at any moment. Putting my sandwich down, I feel my blood start to boil to the surface. I take a gulp of water trying to wash my food down before speaking. I don't take my eyes off his. Clearly he knows I'm pissed. "Are you insinuating this is not a sex club but a whorehouse?" I say this with venom on my tongue.

He puts his hands up. "Whoa, I'm sorry, I didn't mean to offend you. This is not a good second start, is it?"

"No, it's not, and how in the hell can I not be offended by that comment? I mean, look around, do you see the money I have been putting into this place? This is not just a club, it's an experience. An experience like no other for most customers. You see that sex club down the street? It's for members only, and from what I hear, it's dingy and dirty. It's missing the WOW factor that I have created here. My club has an atmosphere for everyone. Have you ever seen a club like this before? Or have you ever been to a sex club in general?" I ask him in a louder than probably required voice.

"No, I have not, so please excuse my ignorance on this. I must live under a rock because I had no idea sex clubs even existed until now. So really, I didn't intend to offend you. I just don't get the concept."

I take a deep breath and try to calm myself. Aunt Gertrude did say most people would not understand so they will be quick to judge.

I rub my temples and respond to him. "It's okay. I'm sorry to blow a gasket. It's just my great aunt Gertrude ran this place in the 40s until it was shut down by the DA. He insisted it was a whorehouse. She told me people would be on a witch hunt even if I did it by the law."

"So let me get this straight, people are going to pay you to go into an open room and have sex with their date and anyone else in the room that is willing. But there are no paid workers that will have sex with them?"

"Yes, I will fire anyone that works for me that has sex in that room with a customer."

"That simply blows my mind. Have you ever been to a place like that before?" he asks, shaking his head in amazement.

All of a sudden, I feel shy about answering him. Why does he care? I dismiss the feeling that something is off and answer the question anyway. "Yes, I have a few times actually," I say, looking directly into his eyes showing no shame.

"Interesting!"

"Is it really?" I respond with a sex-covered tone.

"Yes, it is. Considering I had no knowledge it existed. Who will work the bar in that room?" He asks the question with his eyes on the floor. I wonder if he has the balls to work it. He seems embarrassed.

With a smug smile, I say, "I intended everyone to take turns, but if you can't handle it, I'm sure someone would love to take your shift." I lie to him about his ability to get out of it just to get a rise out of him. "It's the most requested room to work in." I smile and sit back in my chair waiting for his response. Is he going to back out or did he want to be in the room?

He sits up straightening his shoulders in a show of maleness. "I can handle it. I was just asking."

"Good. I will let you have the first two nights in the sex club!"

"Sounds like a plan. I can't wait to check it out." He gets up from the chair, throws his trash in the can next to the door, and turning back toward me, he says, "It was nice having lunch with you. We will have to do this more often." He looks sexy as he leans in my doorway again.

My eyes immediately travel to his cock. Good Lord, he is at full attention and it has my attention. I take my time studying his bulge. It looks to be perfect from here appearing long and thick. Boy, would I love to get my mouth on that. Shit, I have to get it together. I'm the boss, but it's my nature and I can't help it. I take my time raising my eyes slowly to meet his. "Yes, please let's do lunch again. I love the view." He smiles and walks out of my office leaving me wet and frustrated.

CHAPTER 6

Sunny

The last three weeks have been a whirlwind. Leaving St. Louis was fast and stressful. However, I'm pleasantly surprised at how safe and comfortable I feel here. I keep telling myself I should look over my shoulder more often but I don't. I have the security at the club and have been here every day since I was hired a week ago. My time has been spent learning the dances and getting fitted for the elaborate costumes.

Samantha has mixed the old burlesque style with a very glamorous chic New Orleans theme. It shouts class when you walk into the place. Security, yep, the hot security team, not the big fat bouncers I'm used to will be dressed in all black suits like the secret service. I don't know how she did it, but even the bouncers look like models. Our entire staff of workers are beautiful. I feel a bit out of place.

Rumor has it the men hired are gay or refused to sleep with Samantha during their interview. Looking around, I think most are gay other than that nosy Parke and Jackson. Parke is hot but kind of strange. He's always lurking around. He asks way too many questions for my comfort and makes the hair stand up on the back of my neck sometimes. Only Samantha and Shelby know my situation, and he makes me uncomfortable with his over-friendly questions. And if he double-checks with me one more time if I'm a hooker or not, I may punch him in the throat.

And Jackson ... Oh, handsome Jackson. It bothers me to think that he may have slept with Samantha. He can't be gay, and we all heard how Parke refused to do Samantha on her desk, but there has been no mention of Jackson. I was glad to hear Carmella say yesterday that Jackson cut Samantha off in the interview when she started her shit and told her he was the best head of security in the city and he would not fuck around on the job or to get a job. He told her she could hire him now or quit wasting his time. The thought made me smile.

I stand in front of the club again with my mind running wild. This time, my thoughts are thankful reflective thoughts. I think about how far I have come in the last two weeks and how lucky I am to have met Joe and Shelby. Without Joe, I may not be alive. Without Shelby, I would not have this job. And without this job, I would not be daydreaming about the hunk of a man named Jackson. He is insanely gorgeous.

Damn it. What am I doing? Going through what I went through, I should not be concerning myself with another man, no matter how hot he is. *But oh man, is he hot.* And he is hard not to dream about. I felt a connection with him the moment I fell into his arms. But he appears to be a loner, always in the background just watching. He will speak to me if I drum up conversation, but he has never approached me.

Oh well, I don't need that mess right now anyway. I need to stop daydreaming and get to my dressing room for my final fitting. The grand opening is tonight and I'm so excited. All of our costumes are exquisite.

I walk into the dressing room to find Carmella putting the finishing touches on an outfit. She can work magic with anything and everything she touches. She colored my hair and it looks absolutely beautiful.

"Hey, Carmella!" I say with a cheerful tone.

She looks up at me with her infectious smile. Carmella is the most uniquely beautiful person I have ever met. She is short with dyed jet-black hair and pale white skin covered in colorful tattoos. She's a no-nonsense kind of girl. She's very caring but doesn't take shit from anyone, and she will let you know that the moment you meet her. She is in the late thirties but you would never know it by looking at her as she exudes youth.

"Hey! You ready to try on this costume?"

"As ready as I'll ever be. Where's the seamstress?"

"She had Thanksgiving dinner to tend to and said she knew it would fit you so she left it to me to add the finishing touches. So it's just you and me kid. Here, put it on so we can get the hell out of here." She hands me the first outfit. My eyes grow large with excitement.

"VaVaVoom, huh," she yells out.

"You can say that again." I start to get undressed taking the outfit in visually. This is the outfit for the club dance floor. It's an elegant ruby red bodice with black trim enclosed by a corset back. There is an intricate scroll design embossed into the fabric. The top is a sweetheart cut with black ribbon lining the deep plunge. There is also a black sequined design that goes from under the bust down to the bottom. Surprisingly, there are full-coverage panties are attached to the corset. Sewed to the hem are feathers instead of the old time fringe. I point to the bottom of the outfit and hold it up to Carmella.

"This is a surprise," I say.

"What, the feathers?" she questions, looking confused.

"No, the full coverage over the ass."

"That's for the dance club. Samantha was adamant about having distinct sections of the club. And she wanted the dance floor to be a sexy place without it being a strip club. She doesn't want to make women who come to the club uncomfortable.

"Samantha is a genius."

"She really is. I foresee a line around the block to get into this place tonight."

"I sure hope so. I could use the money."

"Can't we all," she says with a smile.

I zip the corset up the side and Carmella strings it up in the back for me. I stand in the mirror and fantasize about going back to school to become a nurse. I always wanted to do that, but Rex refused to allow me to go to college. Meeting him at the young age of eighteen was the worst day of my life. But now I'm twenty-one and free of Rex, I can go back if I want. I will stay in the shelter as long as it takes to save money for my own place and then I'm out of there.

"How is that? Is it too tight?" Carmella asks, pulling me out of my thoughts. I look in the mirror to see a new woman. One that is going to take control of her own life. "It's perfect," I say in awe of my own reflection.

"Oh, wait 'til you see the best part." She pulls out a black saucer hat. It has black and red feather pluming on the top with a black veil that covers my face all the way down to my nose.

"Oh, I love it. And did I mention how much I love the color you dyed my hair?"

"Only a million times," she laughs. "The auburn color looks so natural and sexy on you with those emerald green eyes.

I put my fingers through my long beautiful locks giving her a smile. "Did you know the red you chose is actually my natural color? I have not had my hair this color in years."

"Really? No wonder it's the perfect color for you."

"Yep, when I left the color up to you, I thought you would go black. This color brings me back to a better time in life. I hope to keep it that way."

"Well, this is a good start. You have so much ahead of you. This job pays crazy good money, and you have caught the eye of Mr. Handsome Jackson."

"Shut up!" I swat my hand at her feeling embarrassed. "He's not interested in me." My heart skips a beat hoping he may be interested in me. But he can't be. I can't compare to what he's accustomed to dating. I turn to her and ask, "Is he really? What makes you think so?"

"You were the last hire and Jackson and I were the

first. I have seen the way he interacts with all the girls. They have made more passes at him than they know what to do with in the last two months. But he doesn't budge. He's strictly business with them. But not with you. You don't feel his eyes boring a hole into you constantly?"

I look down fidgeting with my feathers. "I have to admit, I have had a huge crush on him since I crashed into him the day I interviewed. I felt electricity course through me when we collided. I know that sounds stupid," I say, shyly avoiding eye contact with her.

She puts her finger under my chin raising my face to hers. "No, girl, that doesn't sound stupid. I noticed the attraction right away," she says, smiling into my eyes.

"I have been wrapped up in trying to forget the man that did this to me, and I have been too afraid to see it." Tears start to well in my eyes as she looks back at me.

"Oh, honey, you're going to be just fine. Your bruises are almost gone, and we can cover that dragon tattoo you hate with makeup. Light bulb, a light bulb just went off in my head. Do you see it?" She points above her head and continues to yell light bulb.

"No, I don't see it, and you're crazy," I laugh.

"Jackson's sister is a dermatologist. She does laser hair removal, boob jobs, nose jobs, and tattoo removal. You will have to ask him about her.

"That would be kind of weird, don't you think? Hey, sexy, do you think your sister can remove this biker tattoo that was put on my back while I was knocked out on the date rape drug?" Another tear slips from my eye as I realize this is not something I have told Carmella before but it felt so natural.

She puts her hand over her mouth and gasps. "I had no idea. I'm so sorry." She hugs me and doesn't let go, rubbing my back like a mother would do. I have not had a hug like this since my grandmother was alive. And with that, I just lose it and fall into a million pieces.

"Come on, Sunny, talk to me. Let me be here for you. I know we have only known each other for two weeks, but I already feel like you're my little sister," she says softly with her hands now on my shoulders with care and warmth.

Her kindness takes over my soul, and I can see that she really cares. I'm tired of holding it in and hiding it so I tell her everything. I tell her how I met Rex, how I fell for him, how he used to be, and how he took care of my grandmother's burial when I had nothing and no one. Then I tell her about his new dark side, the one that was created by the power of being president of The Flaming Dragons. I realize that I'm now sobbing yet I feel relief.

"Thanks, Carmella, thanks for letting me share this with you. I really needed to get that out to a real friend and not just a counselor."

"That's what I'm here for, honey. Please, anytime you need me, I'm here for you. Look, us southern women stand up for each other. I will beat his ass if he shows his face here." We both belly laugh until I feel the piercing pain of my broken ribs.

"Come on, girl, it's time to get out of here and get our grub on. Where you going for Thanksgiving dinner?" she asks.

"I guess back to the shelter." I shrug.

"Oh no, ma'am. You will not eat dinner at some shelter. You are coming with me. My family has a big crazy dinner with way too much food and lots of fun. Now get dressed before we're late."

"Are you sure? I don't want to impose."

"Yes, I'm sure. You're family now. Move it. My mom gets pissed when I'm late." She smacks my ass as I turn to go get dressed. She is one crazy girl but I know she means it. We are family now.

I get dressed and we get into her car headed out of the city down to the bayou. I watch out the window as the scene changes from close brick buildings to cypress trees and shrimp boats. We pull up to a little wooden house with tons of cars parked out on the lawn and people everywhere. When I get out of the car, Carmella grabs me by the hand dragging me toward the house. She introduces me to everyone, but there's no way I will ever remember everyone's name. They are all so welcoming and the food was to die for. I have never had food this good. I think they had regular turkey there somewhere, I'm sure of it, but I saw nothing that I would consider traditional Thanksgiving food. I did finally come across a turkey, but it was fried and injected with some spicy wonderful sauce that was absolutely amazing. They had things that I have never tasted before or even knew existed: seafood stuffed mirlitons, stuffed artichokes, crawfish pasta, corn and crab soup, and crawfish bread. It all looked delicious, except the raw oysters. I just could not try it, it looked way too slimy. After dinner, I sit and watch everyone laughing and having a great time listening to music and enjoying each other's company. It is so nice to be out of the shelter and act like a normal twenty-one year old. *I have to get out of that shelter soon.*

Oh Lord, I really should not have tried "everything" at Carmella's mom's house earlier. I moan and rub my belly. I'm so full I feel like I could burst. Being it's Thanksgiving, I'm thankful that I'm in the dance club tonight and not in the strip club, and I can pull this belly in tight with my corset outfit. Carmella has finished my makeup and I sit waiting for the doors to open looking at how beautifully she has done my face. I see no traces of my fading bruises. I don't even recognize myself. This is the woman I want to be when I look in the mirror.

Samantha's voice squeals with excitement into the room. "Come on, ladies, get your asses out there and shake what your mamma gave ya! Thanks for everything, girls, without each of you, I would not be able to open the doors with such confidence. Get out there and make me proud," she yells, turning to walk out the door. She seems so genuine, they all do. I try to shake off the feeling of not wanting to get close to them. I want to, I want to let them in as real friends, all of them. But I still have a deep knot in the pit of my stomach that tells me Rex will find me. And when he does, he will destroy anyone close to me. With that thought, my throat starts to feel tight. *I need some air.* I turn and head to the back exit in a hurry while everyone else walks toward the club. I fling open the heavy door and rush out without looking. Bam, I hit a brick wall again. Yep, the brick muscular wall of Jackson.

"We really have to stop running into one another like this," he says, smiling down at me with a hint of lust that I have not allowed myself to see before now.

All the tension I had been feeling seconds ago melts away. My hands are braced on his hard chest looking directly into icy blue eyes. He doesn't say a word. He simply peers back at me. This is unfamiliar territory for me, and I start to get flustered. "I'm sorry. I should have been paying more attention," I mumble.

"No, don't be sorry. I'm enjoying our little run-ins. We have to do this more often. I'm a man of regimen."

His smile is a very sexy half-grin with a gleam to his eyes. I smile back up at him. My lips are so close to his. Oh, how I would love to run my tongue across his lips right now. As I daydream about feeling his warm lips on mine, he leans over and softly kisses the side of my cheek.

"Good luck, Sunshine, you look absolutely gorgeous as always."

Stunned, I don't know how to respond. Before I have a chance, he lets go of me quickly and moves to the door.

Looking back at me over his shoulder as he strides to the door, he says, "Gotta run. We open in two minutes. But don't worry, I will keep a close eye on you." With his signature wink, he's gone and I'm left with a mix of emotions. All I can say is "Wow" as I stand with my feet once again glued to the cobblestone street. Is he really interested in me? What would he want with me? I'm all used up. Rex took everything from me. He broke me down into little pieces until I was nothing. I hear the door open behind me, and turning, I find Carmella staring at me. I can feel it, my eyes are starting to pool, and I don't think I will be able to stop it.

"Don't you dare! Don't you dare smudge my thirty-minute makeup job. Do you hear me? That's an order," she yells. "Now tell me what's wrong without crying. But remember, you have two point two seconds to be on your dancing box."

"Oh, Carmella, I just feel so used up and broken. Will I ever be free of him? Free to be myself?"

"Yes, yes, you will! You're beautiful, funny, and full of life. We will work through this together LATER, I promise. But for right now, you have to suck it up and dance away that bastard. Okay? Can you do that?" she asks.

I shake my head yes because she's right. I need to suck it up and move on. "Thanks, I needed that." With a quick hug, we sprint into the club and reach my box. Before I get on, I see a panicked Samantha walking toward me.

"Oh my God, where were you? I thought you chickened out on me."

"No way, Samantha, I just needed a second to chase away some old memories."

"Are you okay now?"

"Yes, I'm going to be."

"Do you promise to tell me if he comes looking for you? I'm here to help you. I can alert the security team to make sure he doesn't get in."

"No, please I don't want Jackson to know about this or me living at the shelter yet, it's embarrassing. He won't come for me here. He has no idea where I am."

"Okay, but I want to keep you safe from that bastard so let me know if anything changes. And remember your intuition is the best warning sign so listen to it."

"I will, I promise."

She gives me a tight hug and pushes me toward my box. "Now get your ass up there and dance."

I jump up on my box just as the DJ starts to play. The music blares into the room just as the front doors swing open. People start to spill in by droves. I start to dance with my hips moving side to side to the sounds. I throw my head back and lose myself in the music forgetting I'm on display. It's so freeing to be up here. I push the worry of Rex finding me to the back of my mind and get completely lost in the music. As I dance away, I feel a tap on my shoe. Looking down, I see Kitty motioning to me that she's up next and it's time for a break. I climb down and notice Jackson watching me.

I figure what the hell, let's see where this goes. I must be intoxicated by the music and the sensual moves of my body. I run my tongue over my lips keeping my eyes on his watching me running my hands up and down my curves. I give him a sideways grin and turn to walk away toward the back of the club. As I head to the break room, thoughts of him and I together flash before my eyes like a filmstrip. I see him with no shirt and his chest is chiseled to perfection, pure heaven. He reaches his hands out to pull my shirt over my head burying his face in my cleavage. I can almost feel his warm breath on my neck as he turns me around pushing me against the wall. The last image in the movie in my mind is the horrid look on his face when he sees the awful tattoo Rex marred me with. I'm a marked woman. I have to get rid of Rex's branding.

I reach the break room to find Carmella having a drink.

"You looked great up there. Did you have a good

time?"

"I did. I was able to lose myself in the music. But you know, I've been thinking about what you said earlier, and I'm going to ask Jackson if his sister can take a look at my tattoo. I need to get rid of the past and move on."

"I think that's a great idea. You can talk to him tonight at the after party."

"After party? There is an after party? I'm not sure I will be able to keep my eyes open that long."

"Sure you will. We can't have a grand opening without an after party," she says, bouncing up and down with excitement.

"Okay, I will do it then."

"Don't worry, we will get you some liquid courage before you ask. Shots never hurt."

"Oh, I don't know if I should drink."

"Why the hell not? Are you allergic?"

This girl is nuts in a good way. "No, I'm not allergic. I just have not drank in a very long time. Actually, I can't even remember the last time I was allowed to drink."

"Well, you are a big girl now. If you want a drink tonight, you will have one."

"You're right! I think I will have a drink to celebrate the new me in my new life."

I spend the rest of my shift losing myself to visions of a naked Jackson. My shift is over before I know it. Looking up at the clock in the dressing room, I see it's 2:00 a.m. I should be exhausted, but I'm ready to start my new life with my new friends.

I start to undress from my costume and put on the frumpy clothes I picked up at the shelter. Carmella catches me frowning in the mirror.

"We need to do some serious shopping tomorrow with your first night's tips," she yells from across the room. Dixie overhears us and waves me over to her locker.

"You look my size. Feel free to borrow whatever you

want until you get on your feet."

"Are you sure, Dixie?"

"I wouldn't offer if I weren't. This is the best group of girls I've ever worked with, and we're going to be like family. So yes, I'm sure. Take a look and pick something."

I pull her into a hug thanking her. "You pick. I have no clue what's cool. I have been living under a rock for the last few years."

She pulls out a short jean mini skirt with a black halter-top. My eyes get big. I don't think I have the confidence to pull that off. "Oh, Dixie, I don't know? You think I can wear that?"

"What, you don't like it?" she says, upset I don't like her choice.

"No, I love it. I think you would look like a million bucks in it. But I'm not sure I can fill that out right."

"Do you own a mirror, bitch?"

I stare at her blankly hoping she is using the word bitch in an endearing way as she smiles back at me. But I'm still not sure what she's trying to say.

"Sunny, you're hot! We need you to find some self-esteem. You will rock this outfit. Check out these shoes. I hope you are a size seven." She pulls out a pair of high wedge black leather booties with silver studs up the back. "We're going to help you find the real Sunny. You're beautiful and you're worth it. Now put this shit on right now; it's not an option," she scolds with her hands on her hips.

My heart swells with acceptance. I do my best to channel her confidence. Slipping into the skirt, I feel like it was made for me fitting like a glove. It falls about three inches below the roundness of my ass. I pull the shirt over my head, and the halter-top does wonders for my boobs. And these shoes are to die for. Looking into the mirror, I can see it for the first time in years. I pull my auburn locks down from the up-do and shake it out. My red hair is gorgeous and I have to admit I look pretty damn hot in this outfit. I spin around to Dixie and Carmella watching me with crossed arms. They both have an "I told you so" look on their faces.

"Alright, you guys were right. I look okay."

This infuriates Carmella. "I have a problem with both those statements. First of all, it's not you guys, it's y'all. The last time I checked, I don't have a dick, I'm not a dude, so don't call me a guy. Second, you don't look okay. You look fucking smoking hot."

With a smile, I say, "I love y'all."

Carmella grabs me by the hand pulling me all the way to the bar. She yells to the bartender, "Three shots of tequila."

Oh Lord, this is going to be a crazy night. We have a lot of fun dancing and laughing with each other. An hour or so goes by before I realize I have not seen Jackson at the after party. I feel my shoulders slump and a frown crosses my face.

"What the hell is wrong with you now?" Carmella yells over the music. "I told you this sorry for me shit is done with. You have to get it together and toughen up if you are going to run with us."

Her statement should offend me, but I know she means well and she is right. I'm tired of being the victim. I look at her with determination. "I'm going to find him."

"Who?"

"Who else, Jackson, dumb ass," I say, laughing.

"Oh okay, because with that look you just gave me, I thought we were going on a road trip to kick Rex's ass."

I slap her shoulder knowing that is a crazy idea, but it sure did sound good coming out of her mouth. I walk away from her in search of Jackson. Our party has dwindled to just a few of us and I don't see him anywhere. I see Samantha on a bar stool pretty cozy with Parke. I walk toward her not wanting to stand alone.

"Hey, y'all," I say, feeling like a complete moron, and I know I'm blushing. It's just not something I can get used to.

She laughs loudly at me. "You getting shit about using you guys?"

I shake my head yes but change the subject quickly. "Have you seen Jackson?"

"Yeah, have you not? He's been sitting in the back of the room watching you for the last hour." She points to the back.

"Thanks, Samantha, see ya'll later," I say, walking away from them headed to Jackson. I find him sitting at a table alone. He smiles up at me as I approach the table. He stands and pulls out a chair right next to him. From this view, I can see Dixie and Carmella dancing and cutting up.

"Why are you sitting back here all by yourself?" I ask.

He turns to me with his eyes piercing my soul. "I was watching you have fun, watching you let go of what has been holding you down."

I have had quite a few shots and a few drinks by now. I'm amazed by his assessment. "You saw all that from here?"

"You can learn a lot by watching a person when they have no idea they are being watched."

"What are you, a private investigator or something?" I slur. "So what else did you learn?" I ask, not wanting to hear silence.

"I learned you have some ink on that pretty little back of yours that you're no longer comfortable with," he says, taking a sip of his drink and waiting for my response. I don't know how to respond to him. This is what I said I wanted to talk to him about, but I thought it would be on my terms. How could he tell I don't want the tattoo? I feel myself start to cave and retreat when I hear Carmella's voice in my head, *"Suck it up girl and move forward."* And that is exactly what I'm going to do.

"You're a very observant fellow. Yes, I have this crappy tattoo that I actually was coming to talk to you about."

"You want to talk to me about your dragon tattoo?" His eyes are wide with surprise as he thought he had me figured out.

"Yeah." My courage is on its way out so I pick up what he's drinking and take a swig of the brown liquid. When it goes down my throat, it feels like fire. "Good Lord, what the hell is that?"

He chuckles with that sexy grin. "Straight Wild Turkey. I take it you don't like it?"

"Hell no, that's way too strong for me." His drink immediately warms my belly and his lighthearted laugh helps calm my nerves. I do my best to sit up straight and bring my eyes up to meet his. "Back to the tattoo, yes, I wanted to talk to you about it. The girls told me your sister is a dermatologist that specializes in tattoo removal. I was hoping you could give me her number so I could go visit her and get an assessment on getting it removed so I can save up."

He turns his large body toward mine at the table placing his hand on top of mine. The heat I feel from his touch is crazy. I have never felt a reaction from an innocent non-sexual touch before. "I'll give you her number on one condition." *Please let that condition be to lick you from head to toe.*

"What's the condition?" I ask, flinging my long red curls behind my shoulders and revealing the cleavage that is being pushed up in this tight halter-top.

"Tell me what the story is with the tat?"

I pull my hand from his quickly trying to stand as fast as I can to walk away from the table. I'm not ready to do this. I can't tell him the story. He will never be interested in me if I tell him about Rex. As I start to take a step away, I feel his massive arm wrapping around my waist. He pulls me firmly to his body with my back pulled to his hard chest.

I feel his excitement pressed against my ass.

I feel his breath on my neck as I hear his voice. "Hey, I'm sorry. I don't mean to be pushy, but in case you haven't noticed, I'm a loner. I'm not easily impressed by most women." He pauses for a moment looking into my eyes when I turn my face toward his. I see his jaw flinch. "But you, Sunshine, you, I can't take my eyes off of. I've never had a woman affect me like you do. You occupy my thoughts and my dreams, and I don't even know you. I just want to get to know you. I know you want to get to know me Sunshine? I see it in your eyes."

Instead of answering his questions, I start to tell him about the tattoo. "I didn't ask for this tattoo. At a very young age, I was involved with a man that's the president of an MC. Once I realized how bad he was, it was too late. When he felt me pulling away, he slipped me the date rape drug and I woke up with this." I turn away from him twisting my back and pulling up my shirt to reveal the hideous dragon tattoo spread across my lower back like a tramp stamp. I keep myself turned away from him in embarrassment. Above the dragon spitting fire, it reads, "Property of The Flaming Dragons MC."

I feel the fire of his touch. His large hands are now on my bare skin wrapped around my waist with his thumbs rubbing over the tattoo. His long fingers are spread across my belly. I'm sure he's disgusted. Feeling exposed, I pull my shirt down and turn quickly to him, ashamed and looking down not able to meet his eyes.

I feel his hand under my chin pulling my face up to his. "Why are you ashamed? You were marred by evil. That's not your fault. My sister will see you in her office first thing Monday morning, and she will get this taken care of."

"OMG, really? How do you know she has room for me on Monday?"

"She will make room when I give her a call in the

morning. Just be there for 8:00 a.m., okay?" He pulls a card out of his wallet with his sister's information on it. "No one should be tattooed against their will."

I'm overcome by his kindness and shocked he didn't run for the hills. I reach up on my tiptoes to give him a big hug. "Thank you, Jackson, I really appreciate this."

He stares down at me giving me a nod. "Gotta get going. I have an early run in the morning. You need a ride home?"

I feel the blood from my face drain. He can't know I'm staying at the shelter, not yet, not all at once. "I have one, thanks." Slipping the card in my back pocket, I turn and walk away as casually as possible. I have no idea if I succeeded.

CHAPTER 7

Samantha

What a night! I sit at the bar alone taking in how well it went tonight. The girls were amazing, security was flawless, and the sex room was … HOT! I need a stiff drink to get me past the visions of what went on in there. I take a sip of my crown on the rocks and let the images of the night replay in my mind.

The doors open on time with a line of people out on the street. They spill into the club like slow moving lava, pouring into each nook and cranny and heating up the scene. The music blares as everyone dances with the drinks flowing. The energy is unmistakable. The excitement of being in a dance club that has exotic dancers in one room and open sex in the other is electric. I can't help but smile. *This was for you, Aunt Gertrude. I hope you approve.* I smile as I lift my drink up to the heavens and toast her.

I start the night by finding my crew in the VIP section. From across the room, I see Shelby and Grant dancing in their reserved section. The change they have made as a couple is beautiful. They exude love and sex. They are having a great time up there laughing, bumping, and grinding. Shelby has gotten so far out of her shell, sometimes Grant needs to gently nudge her back a bit when she drinks. He tries to rein her in as I approach them. She has him by his ass with her tongue down his throat. He pulls back with a laugh and shakes his finger at her. She looks away shyly as she sees me watching them. I wiggle my way through the crowd to get up to them.

"OMG, Samantha, this is the most awesome club I have ever been to in my life and we have not left this spot," she yells over the music with a giant grin on her face.

I pull her into a hug celebrating this great accomplishment. Without Shelby and Grant's encouragement, I would have never pursued Aunt Gert's dream. I have to admit it quickly became my dream as well, almost as if Aunt Gertrude's soul took over my body.

"Don't go getting all mushy on me, girl. This place is great." She can sense I'm getting a bit emotional, which is not like me. She pulls me close yelling over the music, "I'm working on getting Grant into the sex room. Will my VIP ticket get me into the private room?"

"Girl, you know it will. I really would love it if you all would at least take a tour of the room. It's not like you would be gawkers. You've experienced it before. One of the private rooms is named The Cyber Incident," I say, wiggling my eyebrows up at her.

"No way? You named each room?" she asks as her cheeks start to blush.

"Yes, there are three private rooms, and they each have a theme. The Cyber Incident has a camera stand that's made for smart phones."

"You are filming people having sex?" she gasps in horror.

"No, Shelby, you're so gullible, girl. The stand is there for the couple to put their own phone on and it's in the perfect position to film the bed. I just figured in today's world, everyone's doing it anyway, so I might as well make it fun. You kind of treat it like a photo both. I have some cool movie props in there and you just have a great time."

She stares at me with her big eyes, acting shocked, but I see excitement and curiosity in them.

"Wow, I would have never imagined."

"Maybe the talk of taping it will help you get Grant up there." She slaps at my arm playfully, "I will work on him. How long is this VIP pass good for?"

I can't contain my smile as I yell over the music, "Forever! Have fun on your own time. It doesn't have to be tonight. You two are my very best friends, and you hold the only lifetime membership cards free of charge."

She's the one now jumping up and down in excitement and getting all mushy, hugging me kissing my cheek, and more hugging. "Alright, that's enough, woman. I have to get to work," I say through a smile and push her away.

"Thanks, Samantha, we're having a great time. And I look forward to making this a monthly event. With or without the sex room."

"Good. I know ya'll will have fun. Sorry I have to run, but this place won't run itself. I will try to swing back later."

"Don't worry about us. We're having a great time, and I know you're busy. Go make this place an empire," she yells, shooing me off with her hands.

I run off to check on the exotic dance room. More wall-to-wall people. I'm happy to see my plan of elegant old world chic attracted not only men to this room but couples. There's even a bachelorette party in one corner having a blast. I may have to send Parke over there in a bit to make sure they're not being over served. Just as the thought crosses my mind, the girl with the bride headpiece on jumps up on stage and starts removing her clothing. Before I can panic, Manny the bartender is up and over the bar. All straight women love sexy gay guys. Once she sees Manny reaching for her, she jumps down into his waiting arms and starts to use him as a stripper pole. He guides her back to her table and informs the bunch nicely that they're cut off. Seeing he has the situation under control, I take a deep breath and head back up the spiral staircase to the sex room.

As I ascend the stairs, Maroon Five's *One More Night* bounces off the walls as the scent of sex fills the air. Just the smell alone makes my pussy ache. Once I reach the top of the stairs. I can't help but feel déjà vu. The feeling that I've been here before, or seen this exact scene before, is overwhelming. It takes my breath away to even think her soul has entered mine, but I know she is within me, pushing me to go beyond my comfort zone.

The moans of pleasure are barely audible over the music, but there's no need to hear it when you see it. You can feel the pleasure painted by their motions. This is the first time I've truly missed Phillip. He would have dragged me by my hand and demanded I get on my knees like a good little submissive and have a good time by sucking his cock. And let the truth be told, I really miss that as I look out at the bodies enjoying each other.

The heat you feel when you walk into a sex club never dulls from experience; it only grows hotter. I take a moment to glance over the room already feeling the slick heat between my legs. My eyes can't move away from the couple on the circular entertainment sofa. This section is set up for couples that want to be watched. I have crescent-shaped sofas surrounding the large circular sofa in the middle. While her partner fucks her slow and hard, she's looking into the eyes of a handsome man watching. She keeps her eyes locked with his as she comes. It's too much for me to bear. I have to stay busy. I need it so bad right now, I can't watch any longer. I walk over to the bar only to find more trouble. Parke has been leaning on the bar watching me watch the couple with a smile on his face.

"Oh, wipe that shit-eating grin off your face and give me something stiff."

"I have something stiff for you alright, but did you forget that ridiculous rule you have already? One night of having the sex room open and you're ready to wave the white flag?"

"No, asshole, I'm not giving in. I just need a fucking drink. Can't the owner get a drink without all this crap?" I say, waving my hand in annoyance.

"Yes, ma'am, on its way."

I don't know how long I'm going to be able to hold out. This is torture. I will never tell Parke that, but I really don't think I will last a week. I will have to rethink this rule of mine, because it sucks balls.

"There you go, ma'am, crown on the rocks, stiff enough for you?"

"Perfect. So tell me, Parke, how have you been making out in this room tonight?" I smirk, trying to turn the attention away from me.

He pinches the bridge of his nose and shifts on his feet uneasily, avoiding eye contact. "It's fine," he says, picking up a towel to polish the unused glasses. Here's that damn feeling again. The déjà vu sends chills up my spine. I turn my head to the side trying to focus on the handsome man before me.

"Parke, are you sure we've never met before?"

"Where did that come from? We have known each other for weeks now."

"I just keep getting this feeling that we've met, that we have sat at a bar just like this before. Are you sure you have never been to a sex club before? I'm really beginning to think you may have been at one of the masquerade balls where your true identity would not have been revealed."

"I'm fucking positive. How can anyone forget a scene like this?" His hand waves across the entire room making a spectacle of himself. I grab his hand and put it back on the bar. As soon as my hand touches his, I feel a sear of heat course through my body starting at my fingertips. I quickly drop his hand not wanting to start something I can't stop.

I whisper, "Calm down, Parke, you can't go yelling and pointing at people like that." I look around in hopes no one saw.

Shifting his eyes downward, he says, "Sorry, but this is a bit more intense than I expected. And trust me, I have never been in a sex club before." Closing the space between us, he leans over the bar and his hot breath scorches my damp skin. "Had I known what I was going to see tonight, I would have most certainly set up one my hookup buddies to be ready and waiting at the door at knock-off time."

I blink wanting to escape his heat and the desire in his eyes. I push back off the bar. "Sorry for the blue balls, but you will need to be more prepared next time you work this room." I saunter off giving him one quick sultry glance over my shoulder. *Good Lord, I may need to take a break in my office to release this stress.* Looking down at my watch, I see we only have one hour left until shifts change then things will start to wind down.

Finally the night is done for the first shift. I had told the entire group to meet me in the back of the club where I sectioned off an employees' only after party. Once I arrive, everyone has gathered with drinks in hand. I scan the room looking for Jackson. He is the only one missing. Ah, there he is hiding in the shadows in the back of the room watching Sunny. All my girls look amazing tonight, but I am most shocked with Sunny's transformation. Carmella has really taken to her, helping her with her wardrobe, makeup, hair, and most importantly, self-esteem.

"Thank you, everyone, for an extremely successful grand opening. I could not have done it without you each and every one of you. Drinks are on the house, but don't get crazy. I need your asses back here tomorrow. Enjoy and relax. Y'all deserve it." I walk to the bar for another crown on the rocks as I never did get a minute to hit my office to relieve my stress. *Oh no, and here comes the stress builder.*

"You mind if I sit next to you?"

"Of course not," I say, lying my face off to Parke.

"Look, again I have to tell you I'm sorry. I'm sorry for trying to make you uncomfortable back there in the sex room. Let the truth be told, yes, I was very uncomfortable back there. That's not my cup of tea, yet it was exciting but odd. I assume I will get used to it, right?"

"Sorry to say, but no, you won't. It will always have you high strung, but hey, I'm sure your latest hookup won't mind."

Looking down at his drink, I notice he actually looks a bit embarrassed. "That was a joke. I don't have a hookup on speed dial, so hopefully, I won't have to file a workers comp claim for a carpal tunnel injury on my wrist next week."

I spit my crown across the bar and laugh hysterically. Covering my mouth trying to cover the mess I made with that stupid little napkin you get with a high ball, I look at him as a friend and not as a sex object. "I needed a good laugh. Thanks, Parke."

"I'm glad I could be at your service. You know, I'm really a nice guy if you would get to know me. I know nice guys never go far, but hey, you refuse to go there with me, so we might as well have a good platonic time, right?"

I raise my glass to his. "To a good platonic time." We sit at the bar for over an hour just talking and laughing. It felt so nice, nice to not have the sexual tension. Don't get me wrong, I'm sexually attracted to him, but the no sex rule with our new platonic good time has really helped us both relax and ignore the tension. For once, I'm going to try this get to know a guy thing out.

CHAPTER 8

Sunny

I finally wake up Friday somewhere around 1:00 p.m. remembering I had agreed to go to the mall with Carmella. *I must be nuts going to the mall on Black Friday,* I think as I lift my head off the pillow. But I need better fitting clothes and some basic makeup of my own so I don't have to keep mooching off Carmella. The tips were great last night; I made $450 in cash. And that was just from dancing on a box with all my clothes on. This is going to be a pretty good gig. I love all the girls. They're so welcoming and seem to be truly genuine. After a month or two, I should have enough to move out of the shelter and into my own place. Who knows, maybe sooner! But I don't want to overestimate how much I will make in the exotic room. Carmella offered me her small extra bedroom, which was super sweet of her, but I don't want to impose.

Shit, I told her I would be ready for 1:30. I must have drank a lot to have slept this late with everything going on around me. Most of the women have been up and busy taking care of things, like washing clothes, doing chores, or just hanging out and chatting. I jump out of bed grabbing things to head to the shower. Twenty-five minutes later, I have my frumpy clothes on and I'm out front waiting for Carmella to pick me up.

When I see her car come around the corner, I start to wave and walk to the curb ready to get out of here.

"Hey, chick, you ready to hit the mall and get rid of those crappy clothes?" she asks, waving her hand like a wand up and down my body.

I look down at the dingy borrowed shirt and the jeans that are way too big, "Hell yes, I can't wait. Quit talking and drive, bitch," I say with a smile.

"I'm glad you're coming around. Let's get the hell out

of here."

The mall is not far out of the city into the suburbs. Once we pull into the parking lot, we notice today is probably the worst day to go shopping for clothes. It's packed! *Oh well, a girl's gotta do what a girl's gotta do.* We park in a spot that feels like a million miles away and trudge toward the mall. I keep myself aware as my gut tells me that I'm being watched.

Even though the mall is packed, I am able to find some awesome sales and pick up everything I want and then some. I am a bit disappointed in myself to realize I spent every dime I have. Oh well, I will make more in a few hours I think, allowing a smile to cross my face. Tonight is my first night in the strip club, and I have to admit, I have some butterflies. I'm not sure why though. I'd stripped for a year before getting involved with Rex. I had a fake ID and started work six months before my eighteenth birthday in an effort to try to help Grammy with the bills.

When we pull up at the shelter, I don't know what comes over me, but I can't take it there anymore. They have been extremely nice and helpful, and I'm so thankful for them, but there's no privacy. Without Joe and the shelter, I may not be alive. But it's time to go, time to spread my wings. I turn to Carmella. "You mind if I take you up on that spare bedroom offer?" I say with the saddest puppy eyes I can manage. She squeals and wraps me in a suffocating hug.

"Of course, I can't wait. It's going to be like high school all over again, but this time, I will have a best friend."

"Thanks, Carmella, give me a minute, and I will go grab my bag and say my goodbyes."

"Alright, bitch, I'll be here waiting."

Tonight is my first night in the strip club and it's almost curtain call. I had a shot of tequila before coming out to help settle my nerves. It has not kicked in yet, but the curtain opens anyway. There are three of us on stage, which helps a bit, but my hands are still a little shaky. *Express* by Christina Aguilera blares from the speakers. I throw my head back, close my eyes, and let, the music take over. Opening my eyes, I stare up at the two massive crystal chandeliers above the stage and think about how perfect this song is for the club. It's a burlesque song with a hip-hop vibe and it's sexy as hell. The costumes we have on tonight are old-school burlesque colors of black and red. I have on black striped thigh-highs with red satin bows at the top, ruby red platform heels, and a black skirt trimmed in red lace with a large plume of long red feathers attached to the back of the skirt. The top is intricately beaded rhinestones that shimmer like diamonds from the lights shining down on us. Oh, and how can I forget the top hat and gloves? Samantha loves satin gloves and hats. I have to admit, I'm glad all of the hats have black veils that cover our eyes. We can still be seen, but it's just the level of protection that helps me get comfortable with being on stage.

I take a deep breath. *You can do this, you have done this before, and you know the dance.* I bring my face down to look out at the crowd as we strut to the music. It only takes me a moment before I remember what it feels like to work the crowd. How empowering it is to be in control of their minds and pockets right now. From here on out, I put myself on stripper autopilot. As I move through the song, the clothes come off, and it feels good to be in control of my body and my life. I use this dance to remove Rex from my soul. When the curtain closes, the three of us rush to pick up the money before the next set.

"Hot damn, girl, you rocked it out there," Dixie says,

helping gather our tips. "You didn't even move like that in practice, where did that come from?"

I look up at her and giggle. "I don't know. It just came out. I'm ready to be in control of my life and my body. It just poured out of me."

"It was fucking hot, girl, and it made the money pour right out of their pockets. You're going to kill it during your solo later."

I blush as we rush off stage laughing together and heading back to the dressing room. I'm so stoked with my new confidence I want to celebrate. "Do a shot with me, Dixie?" I demand.

"I don't usually drink when I dance," she says, raising one eyebrow at me.

"Come on, don't be a pussy, just one."

"Did you really just call me a pussy?" she yells.

"I'm sorry. I got carried away. I didn't mean to offend you," I say, looking down and feeling embarrassed. When I look up, she is hysterically laughing at me. "What? What's so funny?"

"You. I'm not offended asswipe, I'm just fucking shocked to hear you call me a pussy. That's something I would call you, not the other way around. But I have to admit, I'm glad our southern charm is rubbing off on you. One shot, I will have one shot with you to celebrate this new assertive you."

I wrap Dixie in a big hug. "Thanks." We do one shot that goes down hot and fast. I'm pumped and ready for my solo, but I have about thirty minutes to wait backstage. I hang out chatting with the girls when Carmella barges in with her typical flare.

"Hey, bitches, y'all ain't fucking up my makeup with all that bumping and grinding up there, are you?"

Her eyes go directly to me. "I'm talking mostly to you, Ms. Sunny? You were unbelievable up there. I almost threw you a twenty, I was so worked up watching you."

"Oh, stop it, don't embarrass me," I snap at her.

"That was nothing to be embarrassed about. You had every man in the room drooling and emptying their wallets. You should see the fucking line at the ATM waiting for your next number."

"You are full of shit. There's no line."

"Go see if there's a line," she giggles as she moves over to me. "Let me check on that tattoo and see how it's making out under the lights and sweat." I turn to let her inspect my back. "Looks good. I'm as good at makeup as you are at stripping baby," she says proudly.

"Yes, you are, but hopefully, we won't have to worry with that too much longer. Monday is my appointment with Jackson's sister and I'm so excited."

The door swings open, and Samantha yells, "Sunshine, you're up in five." The door closes behind her, and I'm ready to feel the power of the music.

As soon as the curtain opens, I see Jackson off to the side of the room. I feel a surge of heat travel from in between my legs to my face. He's so hot standing there all serious leaning on the wall with his arms folded and watching me. The music starts and I dance with my eyes trained on him. Occasionally, I have to pay a bit of attention to the other men as they are the ones throwing me money, but I have a hard time looking away from him. I try to figure out what the look is in his eyes. His eyes are so intense, his emotions are hard to pin down. My number is up and the curtain closes. Dixie runs out to help me pick up my clothes and money.

"That looked like a private show, Sunny," she says under her breath.

"Oh no, is that bad? You think Samantha is going to be mad?"

"No, it was sexy. Every guy there wanted to be Jackson. Did you see the money on the floor? Did you even feel the hands putting hundreds in your G-string?"

I look up at her in shock realizing while I knew where I was and what I was doing, I truly did not feel their hands. Yes, they can put money in our G-strings, but I have to be more aware of the faces out there. I can't just let my guard down like this.

"Shit. No, I didn't, and I have to get my head in the game."

"While it was sexy, yes, you do. You have to remember who in the hell slipped you hundred-dollar bills so you can remember those faces for next time."

The night goes by in a blur. I had a lot of fun dancing and hanging out backstage with the girls. It's 2:00 a.m. and my shift is over. I'm exhausted and anxious at the same time. Tomorrow is my first night in the sex room. I'm not real sure how that will work out. I have never been one to watch porn, and it always made me nervous when people at the club would just have sex right there in front of everyone. There, I could just walk away from it, but here, I'm going to be in a hanging birdcage for two shifts of two hours each.

I sit in the dressing room before the club opens, fidgeting with my nail polish. My stomach rolls with anxiety, and I really don't think I will be able to do this. I look up at the clock on the wall to see it is almost time. The door swings open, and Samantha rushes in with a pissed-off scowl.

"Sorry, girls. I'm sorry to say whoever was working in the sex room tonight, you can go home for the night. The members have expressed concerns about being watched by the dancers when the dancers are not participating. I expressed to them that y'all have signed a confidentiality agreement, but I have received several calls and will have to do a survey of all the members before I make a decision on this. Until then, sorry ladies, it's off limits."

I let out a sigh I didn't realize I was holding in. I feel relieved but then think about the money I will miss out on. I really need the money to help save for school. Just as the thought crosses my mind, Samantha continues to speak.

"I know you all count on your tips to make ends meet, so I have an envelope with each of your names on it with a little something extra from me to help. I will send emails out to the members in the morning and have a plan worked out by Monday. But don't worry. If we don't have girls in the cages, we will work it out. I have had awesome feedback about the box dancing, so I can always add more boxes. I also have had requests for more girls in the exotic room, so no worries, we will work it out."

When Samantha walks out, I turn to Dixie. "I have to admit, I'm glad that was canceled."

"Really, because I was kinda looking forward to it," she replies with a cocky grin, pushing me on the shoulder. "Come on, you have to admit, you were a bit curious, huh?"

"Actually, I can tell you, no, I wasn't. I have been to a few motorcycle parties and that's pretty much what they do." I shiver in disgust thinking of the dirty club and all the skanks that hung around waiting for anyone to hit on them.

"What, what do they do?"

"They just have sex right there whenever it strikes them. And I find it a bit unnerving. But hey, that's just me, to each their own."

"I just wanted to check it out for myself, that's all."

"I understand, girl, but I'm glad I don't have to worry about it tonight. So now what do we do for the rest of the night?"

"We can do a girls' night," she yells, clapping her hands. Just walk around the quarter and bar hop. Come on, it will be fun. Please?"

I roll my eyes at her and smile while we walk back toward our lockers. "Get out of your costume, Sunny, we're going to have some fun tonight."

"Alright, but no strip clubs. Take me to see the city. I want to feel the history."

Carmella walks in in her typical fashion. "What are you hoes doing gabbing over there and not in the cages?"

I look up at her with excited eyes and a wide smile. "Samantha said the members complained about the girls in the cages, as of right now we're on hold. Dixie is taking me on a tour of the French Quarter tonight for a girls' night. You want to come with us?"

"Hell yeah, I'm coming with y'all. I know this great voodoo shop that has the best psychic around."

"A psychic. You don't believe in that stuff, do you, Carmella?"

Dixie chuckles. "We were born and raised here, girl, we all believe in spirits, voodoo, and psychics."

I shake my head at the both of them. "Are you all for real? So you're telling me you believe in ghosts and voodoo dolls?" They shake their heads in confirmation. "This is going to be an interesting night.

CHAPTER 9

After changing out of our costumes and into jeans and a t-shirt, we head out into the night air. The sky is clear and the air is cool.

"What a perfect night to stroll around the city," Dixie says, while I take in the views.

"Okay, so tell me where you're bringing me?"

"Well, let's see, there's so much to see. We can do a voodoo shop and get a voodoo doll of Rex to inflict some pain on him just for fun. Or we can go to a psychic down at Jackson Square? Whatever you want."

"I want to do it all!" I say with wide eyes. Not that I believe in voodoo, but what the heck, when in Rome, do as the Romans do.

Carmella pipes up, "Well, we can't do a damn thing until we get a drink."

"I don't want to sit in a bar," I complain.

"Who said we were gonna sit in a bar? We're going to get a drink and walk around the city."

I look at her in confusion. "How are we going to do that without getting arrested? You can't just walk around with an open container."

"Oh yes, you can. This may be one of the only cities you can do it, but that you can. So what do you want to drink," Carmella ask with her hands planted firmly on her hips as if she has run out of patience.

"I don't know? I want to be an official tourist, so what would I have as a tourist?"

"Hum," Dixie sighs with her finger tapping her cheek. "You would have a hurricane from Pat O'Brian's if you were a tourist."

"Then what are we waiting for? Lead the way. I want a hurricane."

As we make our way to Pat O'Brian's, I take in the atmosphere during the short walk. It's so relaxing. People are carefree and having a lot of fun. Out of nowhere, my breath hitches and I get an uneasy feeling. I start to look around at the faces as we pass them and turn around to see if anyone is following us. Samantha said to listen to my instincts, and right now, they are telling me to be very aware.

I hear Carmella whisper to Dixie, "Walk faster. We are about to lose Sunny. She is getting spooked."

I look over to Carmella with a fake smile. "I just need a drink. I will be fine."

"Did you see something that made you nervous?" Dixie asks just as we reach the bar.

"No, I just feel like someone is following us, I'm sure it's nothing,"

Carmella laughs. "We are being followed, alright. Followed by that group of hot guys back there." She turns and points to a group of guys standing there waving at us.

"You see, I knew I was being followed," I say, laughing to cover the uneasy feeling that still sits in the middle of my chest.

The feeling does just as Carmella said it would do after a few sips of this very powerful hurricane and goes away. Good Lord, this thing is strong, and I'm not sure if I should drink the entire thing. We leave Pat O'Brian's with drinks in hand on our way to the first voodoo shop we come to. I look up at the sign. "The Voodoo Queen," I read aloud. "Come on, guys, this is a bit freaky, don't you think?" They totally ignore me and walk in. I follow them and take in the contents of the store. There are all kinds of weird things hanging from the walls: chicken feet, garlic necklaces, buddy charms, voodoo potions, and last but not least voodoo dolls. They were not kidding me. You can really buy a voodoo doll. I'm looking up at the different dolls when a woman approaches me. I'm thinking she works here by her garb. She's very eccentric looking. She has on a long colorful skirt, tons of bracelets reaching up half her arm, large shiny earrings, and a wrap on her head that encases all her dark braids.

"Can I help you find something?" she asks.

"Oh, I am just looking," I reply shyly.

But you know Carmella is not going to let this go. "Oh hell no, we are not just looking. We came here for a reason so tell the nice lady what you want so she can help you."

"I don't know what I want. "Y'all," I say, stressing their term, "You brought me here. I'm not from here. How am I supposed to know what to buy?"

The voodoo lady puts her hand on my shoulder and shivers run up my spine. She has an aura about her that I can't quite place. She's calming, almost hypnotic, when she speaks.

"*Chère,* tell me what brings you here? Are you looking for love, fortune, success, or revenge?" Her voice is thick with a Cajun accent. I feel as if I have stepped back in time with her. I just stare into her chocolate eyes like a fool not sure what to say.

Before I can answer, Carmella, of course, blurts out, "Revenge! Her ex-boyfriend beat the crap out of her and she lives here now fearing he will find her. We need help making sure he stays away from her forever." She stresses the word forever and gives me the eyes.

Ms. Voodoo Queen looks back to me. I feel her looking into my soul. She reaches down to grab both my hands wrapping them into hers and holding them up in the air between us over our heads. Her eyes close and she makes some weird chanting sounds. I look over to the girls for help, and they are trying hard not to laugh, as I stand helpless in the middle of the store with this crazy lady chanting.

They stop as soon as she starts to speak English. My eyes focus on her and listen to what she has to say with a weird sense of anticipation.

"You need a protection voodoo doll. I see an evil

dragon after you."

I gasp in horror that she said dragon. I try to pull my hands away, but she has a death grip on them. Her eyes open wide and stare back into my soul again.

"He's far away right now, but you have to be alert. Don't let your guard down. If you allow the tiger to help you, good will prevail over evil. But you have to let the tiger in, let him know your soul, child. If you don't allow the tiger into your heart, he can't save you," she whispers to me.

Pulling my hands away, I push them into my pockets feeling the wicked magic on my hands. Her eyes have not moved from mine.

"There is a dragon, correct," she states, not really asking but telling me.

I don't know that I can answer that. I'm in total shock she would even come up with that. Carmella has stepped up with her arm looped around into mine answering for me. "Yes, the asshole we just told you about is in a motorcycle club called The Flaming Dragons. Is he looking for her? Can you see him? Where is he? When will he get here?"

The Voodoo Queen raises her hand to Carmella in an effort to try to stop the questions.

"He is not near but he's looking. I see him looking all over the country following ..." She hesitates and scrunches up her eyebrows as if she can't make sense of it. "Trains, he's following trains." I know exactly what she is talking about, but I don't say a word, trying not to let the girls know how dead on this woman is. I pray she stops talking not sure I want to know more.

"You have to let the tiger into your mind and soul to be safe." She grabs me by the shoulders again, shrugging off Carmella and pulling me close. "Heed my warning, child, I want you to be safe," she says with drama in her voice. Her warning sounds so dramatic it's almost comical, that is unless you know what I know. I try to pretend she's nuts, rolling my eyes to Dixie, when the Voodoo Queen turns away from me to grab a male-looking doll from the rack. She holds it up in the air and mumbles some mumbo-jumbo stuff we don't understand.

Dixie whispers in my ear, "I think she is putting a spell on the doll. You need to listen to her."

I look at Dixie with a look of disbelief. Is she freaking kidding me? I don't know what the hell she is talking about. But they seem to be under her spell so I stay quiet.

Once her spell is done, she places the doll in my hand. "You see this pin right here? Every night, you take this pin and you repeat this chant. Dragon stay away, tiger find me and keep me safe. Do you understand me? I feel danger for you. But I also feel safety in the tiger's arms so make sure you find him."

"Him? The tiger is a him?" I mean really, at this point, I don't know what the hell I should be looking for.

"Yes, he will save you."

"How am I supposed to know who he is?" I ask with a confused look.

"Oh, you will know. He has already found you. You just have not let him in yet."

She places her hand on my forehead, repeats the chant, and then walks away from us.

"Did that really just happen?" I ask the girls with wide eyes and shaky hands.

Dixie is wide eyed and shaking her head. "Hell yes, that just happened. Now let's pay for that doll and head to the cathedral because I feel like we need some holy water after that."

"What? You bring me to a voodoo shop, and NOW you feel like you need holy water. You just had a Voodoo Queen put a spell on me, and now we have to go to church?" I say in disbelief.

Carmella grabs my hand and puts my hurricane she has

been holding back in the other. "Here, just drink up and stick the damn doll every night. I don't think we really should discuss this again. Just do as she says."

I didn't tell the girls about Joe putting my clothes on the train cars so there's no way they could have told her that. Oh shit, this is real. This woman is for freaking real, there's no way she could have known that. My mind races so fast I can't keep up with it. I take long fast pulls off my drink in an attempt to stop my mind. When we get to the famous church, I blurt out, "I need to find the tiger, y'all. Please help me find the tiger," I slur.

I want them to tell me the Voodoo Queen is nuts and just a tourist attraction, but they don't. They actually look a bit frightened for me which makes me worry more, which makes me drink more.

"Come on, a little holy water will make us feel better," Dixie, says.

Carmella does not appear to believe her as she looks at her with a raised eyebrow. "It will make us feel better or burn a hole in our forehead?" she asks with a high-pitched voice we all ignore.

We down the rest of our drinks before we head into the church, which by the way feels really wrong after where we have been, but heck, we have not done a damn thing right yet so why start now.

We walk in quickly as they are about to close for the evening. This church is absolutely beautiful. There are black-and-white checkered marble floors leading up to the altar with old large wooden pews on each side. It's massive. Dixie whispers to me, "Let's get the holy water and go." We are in and out in less than two minutes with wet foreheads from making the sign of the cross with the blessed water.

I have washed off some of the voodoo but still feel a bit uneasy about the entire situation.

"So what now?" I ask the girls, ready to change the

subject and forget what the Voodoo Queen said.

"More hurricanes is what is next," says Carmella, walking away and expecting us to follow her. I think she's a bit spooked as well.

We walk back to Pat O'Brian's without saying a word to each other. Once we make it there and get another drink, we sit at a small table out in the patio area. I look at the girls and shake my finger at them. "I don't want to discuss this voodoo thing again tonight, do you all understand me? I'm over it, I want to drink my drink, then let's find a place to dance and have fun. Okay?"

They both look at me in agreement as they take long pulls from their hurricanes. Once we let half of our second drink sink in, we're ready to move past the weirdness of what has happened.

"We need a picture," Dixie shouts over the music. "It's the thing to do when you come here to get your picture taken in black and white with the Pat O'Brian's logo on it. Come on, we have to do it." She gets up to pay the photographer who's walking around with a camera. We take our picture all smiles as the second hurricane has us feeling good and the memory of the voodoo incident pushes to the back of our minds.

Just as the photographer walks away, two very handsome men come up to our table. The tall sexy one points at Carmella. "Hi, don't I know you from somewhere?"

"They all say that, doll," she counters.

"No, really. My name is Kevin, Kevin Breaux. I think we went to high school together. You went to Lynn Oaks down the road, right?"

Her eyes shift away from him, and for the first time ever, I see a hint of embarrassment on Carmella face. What the heck is that about? She's the most confident person I've ever met.

And there is the Carmella I know. She sits up straight

looking him right in the eyes. "Yep, I sure did go there, and now that you say your name, I sure do remember you. Funny that you would come say hi considering how much of an asshole you were to me back then."

Wow, she really called him out on that. But he doesn't seem fazed by it at all.

"That's the reason I came over. I wanted to apologize for being an asshole and ask for you to forgive my stupid teenage self." He stands tall waiting for her to respond.

She's at a loss for words looking down at her drink. "Yeah, whatever, you're forgiven. Now walk along and go find the rest of our class that you were an ass to."

"Come on, Carmella, I was a stupid kid back then. Please don't be mad. Let me make it up to you. Let me buy you and your friends a drink to prove I'm not an asshole anymore?"

She gets up from the table and looks back at the rest of us. "Sorry, we were just leaving and heading to Cat's Meow for some dancing. If you and your friend would like to follow us there, it's a free world." We get up and follow behind her, and the guys are hot on our heels.

Dixie is attracted to the other guy right away and starts chatting him up while we walk. Kevin is dead set on making up with Carmella, and I feel a bit left out, which gives me time to look around a bit. I still feel as if we're being followed. Once we get to Cat's, I see how crazy it is in there. It's a karaoke bar with large windows open to the street, and everyone is dancing, singing, and just having a great time. Kevin is good as his word with buying us drinks.

After a few more drinks and a few really bad songs on stage, I'm done. Kevin and Carmella are pretty hot and heavy making out, and Dixie is about to put the moves on the friend, John I think is his name. Trying to remember his name makes the room spin. In an instant, I don't feel well. Words won't come out of my mouth and my limbs won't work anymore. Everything goes black.

CHAPTER 10

Jackson

Damn it! I can't believe the girls let her get this wasted. Not only is she ten sheets to the wind, she's about to fucking pass out and they have no clue. Thank God, I decided to follow them when they left the club after hearing they were going to walk around the Quarter with just the three of them. I was hoping things would stay calm after seeing them go into the voodoo shop and church thinking they were just showing Sunny the tourist stuff. But no, they had to go back to Pat O'Brian's for more drinks with two guys in tow.

Noticing Sunny looks a bit out of it, I close in on the group. Just as I move in, Sunny goes down, and I'm able to catch her before she hits the ground. She's out cold. I'm beyond pissed because the other girls don't even notice I have her in my arms. This is exactly why they shouldn't go out without a man.

I literally pick Sunny up and carry her toward Carmella. "What the fuck are you doing?" I scold, feeling the veins popping out in my neck when I yell.

She looks up at me with surprise. "Hey, Jackson. What are you doing here," she slurs.

"Apparently saving Sunny from hitting the floor since you two drunks haven't looked her way for the last thirty minutes."

"Aw, she's fine, Jackson, she's having a good time."

"Carmella, she's not having a good time. She's passed out drunk and I need to make sure she doesn't have alcohol poisoning." Dixie leaves her man to come see what's going on when she sees I'm cradling Sunny in my arms like a child. I look at them both and try to contain my anger. "Have either of you noticed if she has thrown up?" They both shake their heads no like two little schoolgirls.

"I'm sorry, Jackson, I had no idea she couldn't hold her liquor. We all drank the same amount. I swear," Dixie whines.

"Well, don't worry about it now. I have her and I'll take care of her." Turning to walk away, I feel a yank on my shirt, and then Carmella is in my face.

"Oh the hell you are going to take my drunk friend home with you to do God knows what to her."

I have had it with this chick, and I'm about to lose my shit and she won't like it. "Let me tell you something, Carmella," I spit out to her with venom. "I could have taken her without ya'll even knowing where she went. So fuck off. You know me, and you know I won't hurt her. Now back the fuck off because I'm not asking for your permission. You got my number. Give me a call in the morning if you want see how she's feeling."

I turn and walk away. I don't have time for her shit. When we make it to my Jeep, she starts moving when the cold night air hits her face. Shit, why didn't I keep the doors attached to my Jeep today? Damn Louisiana weather, nice and warm during the day then a freezing cold at night. It's going to be fucking difficult to keep her in the vehicle. I sit her in the passenger seat, and she opens her eyes for the first time. "Jackson? What are you doing? Are you saving me from the dragon?" she slurs.

"What dragon, Sunny?"

"The dragon that's after me."

"You drank too much, baby, there's no dragon. I'm gonna take you home to sleep it off. Let's get you strapped in. You gonna stay still in this seat for me?"

"I don't have a home, Jackson, I stay with Carmella."

"I know. I'm not taking you there. I'm taking you to my house."

She reaches up grabbing my shirt into her fist and bringing my face close to hers. Even sloppy-ass drunk, she is beautiful. Her big emerald eyes open and stare into mine.

"You taking me to bed Jackson? I'm not ready to go to bed with you. But I think you are hot."

I chuckle at her admission. "You're letting the alcohol talk. Shhh, let me buckle you in. You take a rest. Let me know if you don't feel well and I'll pull over." Before I make it to the driver's side, she's passed out again. I start the Jeep and keep my hand around her wrist when I'm not shifting. It's only a twenty-minute ride to my house in Slidell, but it feels like two hours making sure she doesn't fall out. We finally make it into the driveway when she announces, "I feel sick."

Now I'm grateful for not having the doors attached as Sunny pukes right from her seat onto the driveway without getting it inside my Jeep. I reach over holding her hair back. Looking down, I see that awful tattoo of hers again. It enrages me that someone would do that her. What kind of man would give his woman the date rape pill to brand her? I reach over and wrap my free hand around her waist rubbing the tattoo with my thumb and promising myself I will find the bastard that did this to her. I will find him and make him pay for what he has done to her.

"How you doing, Sunny? You think you can make it to the house?"

"I don't know. How far is the house?"

"It's right there twenty feet away, don't you see it?"

"I can't see anything right now. It's so dark."

"Hold on to the seat. I'm going to come around and carry you into the house." I take my T-shirt off and hand it to her to wipe her face.

"Thanks, this is so embarrassing. I don't usually drink this much. Thanks for taking care of me," she says, looking up at me with those sexy as fuck helpless eyes.

"Anytime, Sunny, anytime you need me, call me and I will be there for you." I don't wait for her response and reach into the Jeep scooping her up into my arms. She rests her head on my chest, and I get this strange feeling in my gut. My head wants to run as far away from this girl as possible. But my heart has me running to her. What the fuck? I don't listen to my heart; I shouldn't listen to my heart. The last time I did, look where it got me. It got me tangled up with that crazy bitch Norma. My stomach rolls thinking about her and the situation. Just as I'm about to listen to my head, Sunny starts to move in my arms.

Her hand goes up my chest and right over my nipple up to my neck. Lord, her touch is so hot, I feel a trace of heat in her wake. "You're so strong, Jackson. You're always there to catch me before I fall. Thank you, Jackson, thank you for catching me."

I say nothing simply pressing a kiss to the top of her head as a silent acknowledgment. Opening the door, I bring her straight to my bedroom. The spare room is dusty with a dinky mattress. I will let her sleep here and I will take the sofa. I put her down to get a wet cloth to wipe her face and neck down. Pulling off her shoes, I notice her clothes are full of vomit. "Oh Lord, what am I supposed to do with this?" I say, looking up for help and taking a deep breath.

"Sunny, are you awake?" I ask her softly. "Come on, Sunny, I need your help getting out of these clothes. Wake up for me, Sunny."

Fucking nothing; she's dead to the world. As much as I would love to remove her clothes and see her in all her glory, I can't do that to her without her being awake. "Damn it! Okay, Sunny, I'm going to cover you with a bath towel, remove your dirty clothes, and put clean ones on, okay?" Still nothing. I get a pair of clean boxers and a clean T-shirt. It was physically a lot easier than I thought to make the transition. Mentally, I wanted touch her, feel her, be inside of her. *Get your head in the game, man, you know you can't do that. Get her covered up and get the hell out of the room.*

I lie on the sofa for about an hour before starting to drift off. It was hard to do knowing she is lying in my bed.

Just as I drift off to images of her wrapped in my arms, I'm jolted by a blood-curdling scream. Jumping off the sofa, I sprint to her. Flipping the lights, on I see Sunny thrashing around the bed but no one else is there. Her eyes are closed and she's still screaming. What the hell is going on? Nightmare, she must be having a nightmare. Should I wake her? Shit, I don't know what to do. I just do what my heart tells me to do. I get into the bed behind her wrapping my arms around her in an effort to calm her. "It's okay, Sunny, it's me, Jackson. I'm here. You're okay."

"Don't let the dragon get me, Jackson. Please! Do you promise?"

"Yes, I promise, Sunny. I won't let the dragon get you. Shhh, I'm here," I tell her, rubbing her arms and trying to soothe her. Oh God, her skin feels so silky. I feel my cock stirring. *Down, boy, this is not the time to wake up.* But he doesn't listen. The more I rub her arms, she starts to calm down and burrow back into me. Her sweet little ass is pressed right on my cock. This is going to be a long night, and I huff into the air.

For hours, I lie awake holding her while she sleeps. A few times, she starts to whimper but is easily calmed by my voice. She keeps asking if the dragon is gone. What the hell is that about? Is the asshole that tattooed her looking for her? Is she on the run? Is it my business? *Remember, she's just a friend; she's not your woman. Don't start demanding answers in the morning. You will scare her off.*

I catch about two hours of sleep before the sun comes up. Along with the sun coming up so does my cock. I have to get out of the bed. I will go mad lying with her in my arms. She has not whimpered in a while, so I think it's safe for me to leave. I slip out of the bed to make coffee and breakfast.

Sunny

I turn over in bed feeling my head pounding. What the hell happened to me? Where am I? I slowly sit up when it all rushes back to me in mental pictures. I see the Voodoo Queen, the church, the hurricanes, and singing and dancing at Cat's. Oh Lord, that was bad. I sure hope no one has that on video I think as a small smile comes across my face. Then the pictures get fuzzy. I remember hearing Jackson. What the hell was Jackson doing there? I remember throwing up out of his Jeep. I lie back in humiliation pulling the sheets over my face. It's at that moment I realize where I am. The sheets smell all too familiar. I know this smell. It's the smell of Jackson. I pop up again from the bed to look around. Oh Lord, that was way too fast and the room starts to spin. I'm afraid to look down, but when I do, I'm relieved to see I have clothes on, only to be alarmed again when I see they're not mine. I have on a man's T-shirt and boxers, yep, no underwear, just boxers.

This is bad really bad. *Think, Sunny. What the hell happened after throwing up?"* I close my eyes trying to concentrate on the scenes from last night. But the only thing I come up with is nightmares of a dragon. The nightmares stopped when the tiger came to save me. Thanks to the Voodoo Queen, I dreamed about a tiger keeping me wrapped safely in his arms. A mother-freaking tiger. Damn it, I need some coffee.

I swing my feet out of the bed slowly trying not to start the spinning again. Looking around, I can tell this is Jackson's bedroom. It's manly and mostly bare. It's very neat with a few items on the wall, all of which are weapons. There's a sword display and some guns that appear to be antique. I get up the strength to get up when I see a picture on the bookcase of Jackson and a beautiful woman. She's stunning. She's almost as tall as he is with a matching skin tone and hair, but she has dark eyes. Her arms are wrapped around his waist with his around her shoulders. The look of love in their eyes sends a spike of jealousy to my heart. I'm sure I would have known if he has a girlfriend, right? I can't look at it anymore. I turn away and head to what I hope is the bathroom.

I open to door to find an all-white bathroom with an oversized shower. It takes up half the bathroom with a long bench and about ten different sprayers coming from the wall. I look down to see there's a new toothbrush on the counter with a note.

I hope you are feeling better. Coffee and breakfast will be ready whenever you are. The sweet note warms my heart and pushes the photo out of my head for now.

I take my time washing my face and brushing my teeth before I get up enough courage to walk out to see Jackson. I feel a bit exposed. You can almost see though the white T-shirt and the boxers are a bit loose on me.

I head out of his room following the smell of coffee and the sound of pots and pans. When I round the corner, I see him standing at the stove. His kitchen is amazing. It's fit for a professional chef. I stand in the doorway watching him for a moment. He has on grey sweatpants hung low on his waist. My eyes travel up to the muscles flexing on his uncovered back. Holy hell, he's hotter than I could have ever imagined.

When he turns around to greet me, I almost pass out. I see an image tattooed in vivid color across one side of his chest, all the blood drains from my face. I feel light headed and lean against the wall for support. The room starts to dim as I see Jackson stride quickly toward me catching me again before I hit the ground.

"Sunny, Sunny, can you hear me?"

I blink up at him staring at the tattoo with the Voodoo Queen's voice replaying in my head. "I'm sorry, Jackson, I must have gotten up too fast." He helps me up guiding me to the farm table near the large picture window. He leans over me to place me in the chair, but I can't take my eyes off the tattoo. Without a proper thought, I raise my hand gliding my fingers across it. Looking up into his concerned eyes, I mutter quietly, "Its a tiger."

Yep the man of my dreams has a freaking tiger tattooed across the entire left side of his chest. It's the most beautifully colored tattoo I've ever seen. It's orange with black stripes. The hair on the tiger looks so real. It's the tiger's face only with its mouth wide open baring its teeth in a fierce growl. The eyes are the same blue as Jackson's.

"This is the most amazing tattoo I have ever seen," I sigh. I don't realize I'm still rubbing my fingers across his bare skin until I see the hungry gaze cross his face with his jaw flinching as he tries to control himself.

I let my hand slip up his chest and around his neck pulling him to me. Without losing focus on his eyes, I press my lips to his while he stares back at me. I shut my eyes and let him take control of my mouth feeling his soft lips press against mine. I open my lips giving him access. I shiver when I feel his hand at the nape of my neck grasping a handful of my messy morning hair. The kiss is hard and full of lust igniting sparks within my body. My heart is pounding in my ears while my nipples pebble under his shirt along with wetness pooling in between my legs soaking his boxers.

It's been so long since I have wanted a man like I want Jackson in this moment. I've never felt this spark with Rex or anyone else for that matter. My belly is warm and my mind is mush.

My world comes crashing in on me when he pulls me back with the hand in my hair. My chin is angled up at him. Gazing into his eyes, I no longer see the hunger but only conflict. I feel my face flush in horror and embarrassment. Before I can push away, he senses what I'm feeling.

"Sunny, this is going to be the most difficult thing I've ever done, but we have to stop," he says in a low voice, not making eye contact with me.

I push him back, jump to my feet, and head back to the bedroom to find my things. I turn to walk away apologizing with my back to him, "Sorry, Jackson, that was my bad. I shouldn't have assumed that just because I woke up in your bed in your clothes that you gave a shit about me." Before the sentence is fully out of my mouth, his strong grip is on my arm and I'm spun around and pinned up against the wall. My heart races as I have a flashback of Rex, but when Jackson's eyes meet mine, my fear washes away. He's not going to harm me. I see anger in his eyes but I don't feel threatened.

"Woman, what the hell is wrong with you?" he asks with a hoarse voice. "If you would've given me a chance to finish my sentence, you would have heard me say we have to stop because I want to get to know you," he says, putting his hand on my face and rubbing his thumb across my cheek. "I don't want to take advantage of you. I feel something for you that I've never felt for anyone." He shakes his head and gives me a chuckle. "That would have been the gentlemanly way to put it, but now that you've pushed me, I'm going to tell you what is really going through my mind. I want nothing more than to spread you across that kitchen table and taste you. I want to bury my hardness deep within you and hear you moan my name and beg for more when you come."

I let out a sigh unaware I had been holding my breath. He's towering over me now bracing both hands on the wall behind my head.

"Woman, don't do this to me. Don't look at me with want and make sounds like that, or I will have to take you right here."

"So how do you propose we get to know each other?" I ask.

His features soften and a sexy smile spreads across his face along with a bashful look. His eyes shift to the floor, and he lowers his hands to my shoulders.

"I don't know. Maybe go on a date. I want to know everything about you. I don't know where you're from, what's your favorite food, nothing. I only know that you are running from a man I despise and that's it. I need more, Sunny."

I smile up at him in surprise that this big mound of muscles wants to go out on a date, a date with me.

"A date? You want to go out on a date with me? When and where?"

"I'll pick you up from my sister's office after your appointment, and we can head out to the shooting range from there."

My eyes narrow not certain I heard him correctly.

"What the hell? A shooting range? That's not a date, Jackson. I'm not sure what girls down here do, but newsflash, that's not a date. A date is dinner and a movie."

He cuts me off by raising his large hand to my face and placing his finger over my lips.

"Shhh, I will feed you after we shoot off a few rounds."

I look down in embarrassment. I'm petrified of guns. I whisper, "I'm scared of guns, Jackson." I look up at him. "Really scared as in I completely freeze and can't move when I see them."

"Don't worry. You're safe with me. I will take care of you. You need to lean to protect yourself, Sunny."

"Protect me from what if I have you to keep me safe?" I whine.

"I can't be with you every second, and if Rex comes for you and I'm not there, you need to be able to take care of it."

"Take care of it as in shoot him. I can't do that." I shrug out of his grasp and head back to the bedroom with him hot on my heels. I reach the room and see my clothes have been washed, folded, and placed at the end of the bed. I turn on my heels only to have Jackson crash into me yet again. And yet again, he catches me in his strong arms.

"You washed my clothes?" I ask in surprise. I have never had any man do anything like this for me. It's always my job to do for them. I've only been taken from not given to.

"Well, of course, I washed your clothes. They were a bit dirty from the vomiting, if you recall."

I put my hands up to my face shielding myself from his eyes. "Oh geez, yes, it is all coming back to me."

His arms are now wrapped around my waist. "Sunny, go on a date with me. I need to learn more about you, and you need to learn more about me. I may be a big man, but my mother taught me manners, and you may be surprised by what my idea of keeping a woman happy is."

I don't even take time to consider. I would be a fool to say no.

"Okay, I will go on a date with you to the gun place but at your own risk. I have warned you that I'm scared, as in mortified, so if you think you can work with that, then it's on."

"Oh, it's on, girl," he says, leaning over and letting his hot breath spread over my ear. "Now get dressed before my manners go out the window. I can't bear seeing you in my clothes for another moment without coming undone." He pulls me in pressing his lips on my forehead. I feel his large erection pressed across my belly, and I can't help it but smile. "Thanks for trusting me," he says, walking out of the door.

I get dressed and find my way back out to the kitchen. Jackson has set the table and is waiting for me to start breakfast.

"Wow, that's a lot of food," I gasp looking at the feast he has set out. There's a large bowl of scrambled eggs, toast, waffles, fresh fruit, orange juice, milk, and coffee.

He stands pulling out a chair for me. With his breath hot on my face again, he says, "This is exactly why we need to get to know each other. I don't like to waste food so I will have to eat what you don't." Grinning up at him, I take my seat.

"Well, let's start getting to know one another, Jackson. I don't drink milk or orange juice. I prefer grape juice, water, or coffee. I love waffles, and veggie omelets are my favorite eggs." Pleased with my sharing, I ask him in return, "What are your favorite breakfast foods."

"I eat everything and anything but mushrooms. So everything you see here at this table I love or would love to eat," he says with a wink.

His gaze is hot on me, and I don't think he is talking about food anymore. I shift my eyes down to find a plate and fill it with the wonderful smelling food.

"So where exactly are we? It's safe to say I don't remember my ride here, and by looking out the windows, it doesn't appear we are in the French Quarter anymore."

"Sorry about that, but you were out of it, and your girls were not keeping an eye on you. Not a good situation in this city or in your position. I don't know enough about what haunts you at night, and trust me, after last night, I know something is haunting you," he says, staring into my eyes.

I shove a forkful of waffles in my mouth, avoiding the sear of his gaze. He wants me to give him more information, and I'm not sure that I'm ready. After chewing, I realize he is still waiting for a response. I have to give him something. "Look, this is hard for me, and it's going to take time and trust for me to let you in. So that's all I'm asking you is not to push me." I keep my eyes down on the table. It's not the woman I ever wanted to be. As a child, I dreamed of being a strong woman, a woman in control of my life. I look up in surprise when I feel his touch. His hand is over mine gently stroking it while I had checked out of the conversation.

"It's okay, Sunny, I'll do my best not to push. But it's my personality to just handle things and get it done. So let me know when I'm pushing too hard and I'll back off."

I look up to see the gentle giant beside me. "I will let you know. But just know he's not looking for me, so you don't have to worry. There is no way for him to know I am here." The Voodoo Queen's words rush back to me.

Let the tiger in. Let him know your soul, child. If you don't allow the tiger into your heart, he can't save you"

He nods his head in confirmation, but I don't think I have convinced him.

"Just a word of advice, Sunny, don't drink that much if you're not with me."

A little red flag goes off in my head. Did he just tell me what to do? This is not the type of relationship I want to be in again. I throw my napkin down on the table and stand. Looking him square in the eyes with a loud clear voice, I say, "I will not be told what to do. Let's get this straight right here and right now. If it is your MO to order women around, I'm out. I will not do this again."

He smirks at me. "Babe, I was not telling you what to do. Did you miss the key words?"

"What are you talking about? You just told me not to go out and drink without you."

"No, I just said a word of advice is not to drink too much without me." *Note to self: Rex was possessive, controlling, and he hurt her physically. I will kill that motherfucker when I find him. If it's the last thing I do, I will find him.*

"I get a little tense when people think they can tell me what to do so I had to clear that up."

"Forget about it, it's all good." He motions for me to sit back down. "Finish your food. You need the nutrition after last night."

I chuckle. "Are you telling me what to do?"

"Yes, at this moment, I'm telling you to eat. Got a problem with that?"

"No, but only because I'm starving." We sit in comfortable silence for the rest of the meal. I take the time to reflect on how different it is when Jackson tells me what to do. It's out of care and concern and not to be in charge of me.

"That was the best breakfast I've had in years. Probably since my grandmother passed away."

"I'm glad you enjoyed it, and I'm sorry to hear about you grandmother. Do you have any other family?"

"Let me help you clean the kitchen," I say, turning away from him. I start to wash dishes and give him some of my family background while I stay distracted.

"I never met my dad. He left my mom when he found out she was pregnant and wouldn't have an abortion. He was twenty-five, and she was barely eighteen. I always admired her for the decision to keep me and to do it alone. She did have my grandmother so she really was never alone. But when I was ten, she died."

I feel a tear slip down my cheek as I look out the window at the boats passing in the canal.

"She was hit by a drunk driver while crossing the street going to her second job. She was a wonderful mother. Even though I was only ten, I remember her oh so well." I drift off into the memory of my mother, her soft kind face, and the amount of love I felt from her. I feel Jackson's warmth on my back.

"I'm sorry, Sunny."

I turn to him and he wraps me in comfort. My face rests on his strong hard chest as he strokes my back.

"Don't worry with the dishes. Let me take you home so you can get some rest before your visit with my sister tomorrow."

"Okay, but we got so distracted you never did tell me where we are."

"We're just outside of the city in Slidell. I have a small apartment in the Quarter for the days it's too late to drive out here. But this is where I can relax." He pulls away from me grabbing my hand and leading me to the back of the house. He opens the sliding glass door to the large wooden deck.

"Wow, this is beautiful. Does the deck go all the way out to the water? Is that your boat? What waterway is this?" I giggle as I realize the barrage of questions I've just thrown at him.

He chuckles at me as well. "Yes, the deck goes all the way out to the water and that is my boat," he says, pointing to the boat at the end of the deck. This is a canal that leads to Lake Pontchartrain. I love it here. It's quiet and peaceful. I can go fishing, crabbing, or shrimping whenever I want. Whatever the season, I can do it all from here, and it's away from the hustle and bustle of the city."

"I can see how this would be relaxing after working four days straight at the club."

"Do you like boats?"

Oh geez, now I have to tell him I'm a scaredy-cat with boats too. Smiling up at him, I say, "I have never been on a boat before. I'm not sure that I'm fond of them."

"Can you swim?"

"Well, of course, can't everyone?"

"No, Sunny, not everyone can swim. I mean, around these parts, 99.9% of people can swim, but when it comes to taking someone on your boat, it's an important question."

"Yes, I can swim but not sure I would like to be on a boat."

"You will learn to love it. That will be our second date."

"You and these crazy dates. The gun place and a ride on a boat."

"It's a gun range not the gun place."

"Yeah, yeah, the gun range and then on your silly little boat, but after that, you have to take me on a real girl date."

He moves forward closing the space between us. Pushing a stray piece of hair behind my ear, he looks at me with a lethal, panty-melting stare. "You go on my two manly dates without complaining, and then we can go on your girly date. I'm a man of my word so make sure there's no whining and complaining on my guy date."

"Deal," I say, his eyes not moving from mine. His hands move to my waist pulling my body flush against the hardness of his body. Dropping his head, he plants those gorgeous lips on mine. They are warm and firm. I open mine to let him in, let him take control. This kiss is different than the one we shared in the kitchen. This one is controlled and tender. His taste is so unique, I can't even begin to explain it. It simply taste like Jackson Devereaux. He gently pulls away and kisses the tip of my nose.

"Deal, now let's get you home so you can rest up for your appointment tomorrow."

CHAPTER 11

Sunny

Jackson drops me off at the apartment I now share with Carmella. Opening the door to the small-bricked building, I find Carmella sitting on the sofa with her hands over her face looking like a train wreck.

"Hey, I'm home. Are you okay? You don't look so well," I say from the doorway.

"I feel like shit. Drank way too much. Never mind me, tell me about your night with the elusive Mr. Jackson Devereaux. And I want all the juicy details."

I walk around to the sofa and plop down next to her. "He is the perfect man, Carmella. It scares me that those words can even come out of my mouth so soon, but he is just perfect. If he has a flaw, I'm missing it."

"What we call that down here is skeletons in the closet. I don't know of any, but I have only known him a short time as well. If I did, you know I would have told you by now, but he is stealth to say the least. Until you, he didn't mingle with anyone else. Check with Samantha. Maybe she has some scoop on him."

"Yeah, maybe I will ask her. Not sure I want to find any bones much less a full skeleton, if you know what I mean."

Carmella struggles to sit up and puts her arm around me. "I know what you mean, but I don't want you to get hurt so we need to know. I will check with Samantha and that sneaky Parke. I'm sure if there is something to know he would know."

I look up at her scared to admit this out loud because of how wrong I have been in the past. "I feel it in my heart that he's a good man, Carmella. Is that wrong?"

"No, sweetie, I'm sure he is. But it doesn't hurt to ask. Don't worry with it. I will take care of it. But I agree. I think he is a good guy. But I think you are changing the subject. Did you do the deed with Jackson or not?"

"OMG, Carmella! I would never kiss and tell."

"He is so hot. If I kissed him, I would rent a fucking billboard to tell everyone."

I can't help but laugh at her because the girl is freaking serious. "No, we did not do the deed, but we are going on a date tomorrow."

"What the hell? He pulled a caveman on me and carried you out of Cat's and didn't have the decency to sleep with you?"

"As much as I understand your issue with that, Carmella, he said he wants to get to know me. And you know, I don't think I have ever gone a real date in my adult life so I am going to give it a try."

"So where are you going on this date?"

I shake my head and laugh out loud. "I guess the real date is up for debate."

She looks at me as if I have two heads. "He is taking me to the, what did he call it? Oh, the gun range?" I sit and wait for her to have the same response as I did.

"And ... what is the problem with that?"

"Oh Lord, it must be a southern thing. I did not think that was a date."

"Yes, girl, out here that's a date. I'm sure he will feed you after he teaches you how to shoot so that's a date. You participate in an activity together then you will share a meal. What else are you looking for? Don't go getting all fancy on Jackson because I don't think that is his forte."

"I wouldn't say fancy, but a nice dinner is what I equate to a date. But I'm going to try and step out of my comfort zone. Anyway, date two will be on his boat, and if I make it through that date without what he calls whining, I get to pick the next date and it can be as fancy as I like."

"Wow! He gave you all that? Well, hot damn, I think you made out better than doing the deed, sister. He's really into you."

"You think so?"

"Hell yes, I know so."

I look up at her with shy eyes not sure I should tell her, but I feel like I have to tell someone. "Carmella," I say quietly.

"Yeah," she says, looking at the television while she flips the stations.

"He has a giant tiger tattoo on his chest." Biting my lip, I wait for her response.

She turns to me with big eyes and her mouth hangs wide open. "Get the fuck out of here. Are you serious?"

I put my hand up to swear. "I'm serious."

"The Voodoo Queen was right." She turns to me grabbing my hands and squeezing. "He is meant for you. You have to let him into your soul. That's what she said, right?"

I shake my head at her wanting to change the subject.

"Enough about me. How was your night with Kevin?" I say, wiggling my eyebrows at her.

She throws herself back down on the sofa covering her head with the nearest pillow. "Oh Lord, Kevin. I thought I left him in my past years ago. I had the biggest crush on him in high school, and he never looked my way. But don't you worry, I made him work for that shit last night."

"Carmella! Did you do the deed?"

"Hell yes! Did you not see the billboard outside?"

"Details, details."

She jackknives up off the sofa almost hitting me in the face.

"Girl, it was so good. That's what I can remember."

"You can't remember?"

"Well, I had a lot to drink. I remember Jackson carrying you off like a caveman. I about wet my pants when he did that it was so fucking hot. After that, I devoured Kevin on the dance floor. I was all over his ass. He asked me if I wanted to go back to his hotel room, and I was game."

"Do you really know this guy well enough to go to his hotel room?"

She gives me an "are you kidding me" look and replies, "Says the girl who had no clue a man picked her up and brought her God knows where?"

"Point taken. Now get to the good stuff." I roll my eyes at her.

"His fucking cock is pierced. Pierced! Have you ever done it with a dick like that?"

I laugh at her shaking my head no.

"Well, I'm here to tell you to find a cock that is pierced and do it."

"You are a mess."

"When that metal ball hits you in places you had no idea existed, it's ecstasy. Kevin is much hotter than he was in school, but now I have to go on a date with him to see if he's still an asshole. I'm getting too old for this one-night stand shit so pray for me that he's not an asshole anymore."

"Will do, my friend. I'm exhausted from last night so I'm headed to bed."

"Bed? Its 5:00 p.m.?"

"Girl, you have no idea how exhausting it is to NOT do the deed with Jackson. I'm physically and mentally drained. I have to be at his sisters office at 8:00 a.m. sharp tomorrow morning."

"Oh yeah, I forgot about that. Okay, girlie, sweet dreams and good luck with the tattoo thing tomorrow."

CHAPTER 12

Sunny

I wake up super early Monday morning both refreshed and nervous. How will Jackson's sister look at me? Who does she think I am to him? One of his flings? I sit up and swing my feet to the floor feeling the coolness of the wood floor on my feet. The sun is just coming up outside my window. I stand at the window looking out at the new city I now call home and decide to forge ahead in my life without reservations. Stretching my arms over my head, I decide that's exactly what I'm going to do. I'll take it as it comes starting with removing Rex from my life.

It's a beautiful crisp fall day in New Orleans. The sun is bright, the sky is blue, and the air is cool. I walk to Ms. Devereux's office since it's not far from our apartment. The city is alive this morning with delivery trucks at every restaurant and employees hosing the remnants of last night's parties out into drain.

In no time, I reach her office building. *Time to get your life back.* I can't stop smiling. I'm ready to move on. Opening that door gives me a sense of strength and power I've never felt before and I like it. I want to be in control of my life and I will.

I flip through the local gossip magazines while I wait to be called.

"Ms. Sunny Walker, the doctor will see you now."

I follow the nurse back to the room where she gives me instructions. "Remove your clothing and put on this paper gown opening to the tattoo you want removed. Mrs. Devereaux will be in to see you shortly."

Mrs. Devereaux? Her card and window said Ms.; is she Jackson's sister? How can she have the same last name and be a Mrs.? I guess it's none of my business and shrug.

After changing, I sit and wait nervously on the paper-covered table. I hear a knock at the door, and it opens to reveal a stunning woman. She is a carbon copy of Jackson but female. She has the same olive skin, matching chocolate brown hair, and is clearly over 5'10" in height with her three-inch heels on. I just can't get over how much they look alike, except for their eyes; hers are brown. Ah, she is the woman in the picture. I smile up at her as she speaks.

"Nice to meet you, Sunny. I take it by the look on your face my brother didn't mention I was his twin sister?"

Shaking my head in realization of the resemblance, I ask, "How did you know?"

"Because the big muscle head never wants to admit he has a twin sister. And you look like you saw a ghost."

I giggle trying to not look like a total idiot. "I'm sorry. I just did not expect his sister to look so much like him. You're beautiful."

"Well, thank you. He gets his looks from me. I'm five minutes older, so don't let him tell you he's my big brother," she says with a smile.

"So tell me a little bit about your tattoo and why you want it removed. I received a text from my bossy brother telling me you would be here and that your tattoo fits my pro bono program and to take extra special care of you." She's now looking at me with a questioning grin.

"Well, long story short, I was involved with a guy in a motorcycle club, and when he felt me pulling away from him, he slipped me the date rape drug one night and had his buddy brand me with the club tattoo bearing his name." I feel downright mortified right now. I mean really, who allows this to happen to themselves?

My head jerks up in surprise when I hear her say, "Fucking bastards. What the hell is wrong with these Goddamn MC clubs? They think they can just do whatever they want, and it's really pissing me off. She steps closer to me putting her hand over mine. "I want you to know you are not the first person I have had in here with the same exact issue."

I look up into her caring eyes as she continues to speak. "I will do everything in my ability to wipe this asshole's mark off your beautiful body."

"Thanks, Mrs. Devereaux," I say, placing my hand over hers and squeezing in appreciation.

"Please call me Melinda. Mrs. Devereaux is my mother. I graduated before I got married and didn't want to bother changing my name on my license so this is what I'm stuck with. And don't consider me your doctor, consider me your friend. Anyone that is a friend of Jackson's is a friend of mine."

I look up at her with some concern. "Exactly how many friends does Jackson send your way?" Yeah, the insecure Sunny is coming out of me but I can't help it. I really don't know this guy, and I need to know if he's a fixer or if he's really interested in me.

Melinda erupts in a deep belly laugh, which confuses me. She's now waving her hand at me to wait since she can't stop laughing. She finally pulls herself together wiping the tears of laughter from her face.

"Oh, honey, you have no idea how much my brother likes you, do you?"

I shyly look down into my lap clutching my hands together. "I am sorry to say I really don't know much about your brother. I literally ran into him when I interviewed for my job, and we have connected, but we have not had a lot of time to get to know each other."

"Well, let me tell you this. Jackson has never, and when I say never, I mean, has NEVER sent someone to me to have a tattoo removed. I will go a bit further and tell you it has been over a year since I've seen Jackson interested in a woman, and I'm excited to see him come alive again."

Looking up at her with big eyes, I say, "Really?" I was unsure if I was just another notch on his belt so to hear her say that gave me butterflies in my belly.

"Uh, really. For him to ask me to do this for you is big for him so know he has some interest in you."

I can't stop smiling. Melinda goes over all the details of how the procedure will work, how it will feel, and how many times it needs to be done, and I hear none of it. Instead, I keep hearing her say over and over that Jackson has to be interested in me.

"By that look on your face, I'm going to assume you did not hear a word I said other than Jackson likes you."

"Is it that obvious?"

Laughing and shaking her head in confirmation, she says, "Yes, it is. But that's okay. He's a pretty good-looking guy so I'll give you a pass on that. But only if you give me all the scoop on him. And I don't mean any gross stuff. Remember, my brother, but he does not tell me much, and for gawd's sake, I'm his twin. I need to know what's going on with him. Turn over and you can tell me everything while I work."

I turn over on my belly to give her access to my hideous tattoo while I say, "Well, I have to admit, I really don't know much about him other than he keeps catching me when I fall."

"Yeah, he's always been a sucker for a damsel in distress."

"We are going on a date after this appointment. And when I say date, I use that term very loosely. I'm not sure Jackson knows what a date is."

"Let me guess. He is either taking you on his boat or to the shooting range."

I turn my head back to her in surprise. "Is that an acceptable date down here?"

"I wouldn't say for down here in general, but if you want to date or get to know Jackson Devereaux, then that's what you are going to get."

With that, she starts zapping at my tattoo. It takes

about thirty minutes for her to complete the first session with five more secessions to go. The time passes quickly with her telling me some really cute stories of Jackson as a child. Once she is done, she uses her phone to snap a picture of my tattoo to show me the change.

Seeing the image makes me feel a little piece of what Rex destroyed in my soul has returned. It's an amazing feeling. "Melinda," I gasp, "You removed the words first?"

"Well, of course, I did. He's not entitled to have a hold on you, Sunny, and you're nobody's property."

I sit up quickly and wrap her in a hug.

"I could never thank you enough for this, and once I have some money, I want to repay you for this."

"Oh no, ma'am, you will not pay me for this. This is what I do. I make a lot of money from the rich vain society of New Orleans, and I dedicate a certain percentage of that to cases like this. Not all are the same, but it gives me more gratification to remove this tattoo than it does to make Mrs. Robichoiux's boobs three times too big when her husband is cheating on her with someone twenty years younger anyway. Now get dressed and I will meet you at the front desk so you can make the rest of your appointments."

I start to tell her thank you, and she swats my words away with her hand and walks out of the room. I laugh out loud when I hear the nurse call, "Mrs. Robichoiux to the next available waiting room please."

I look up and say a silent prayer in my head. *Thank you, God for putting these wonderful people in my path.*

When I walk out of the room and turn the corner heading to the counter, I see him. He literally makes my heart skip. He's leaning on the counter with his ankles crossed and standing next to his sister smiling, laughing, and looking at her with such love. Before they realize I'm there, he pulls her into a hug and kisses the top of her head. She laughs and pushes him away not wanting to look too mushy with him.

Melinda sees me watching and calls me over.

"Come on, Sunny, come make the next five appointments with Dr. Pain," she laughs.

"I have to admit, it didn't hurt that bad."

"Really?" she asks surprised.

"Maybe I just didn't feel it as I was distracted by stories of Jackson and his teddy bear." Jackson's look of affection for his sister turns into daggers.

"You did not?"

"Oh, little brother, you may be bigger, but you always seem to forget I'm still the big sister. It's my job to tell embarrassing stories of you as a child."

"Melinda, you are five minutes older. I have told you time and time again that I let you out first because it was the gentlemanly thing to do." He lets a small smile spread across his face.

"Yeah, yeah, yeah, whatever you say, little brother."

"Make her appointments so we can get the hell out of here. I hate doctors' offices."

"Want me to give you a shot?" she teases.

I make my appointments and say a quick goodbye to Melinda as Jackson pulls me out of the office by my hand. Once we're out on the street, he turns to me. "Did I mention my sister was a twin and a pain in the ass?"

"Nope, you never mentioned your sister was a twin. And she is not a pain in the ass. She is super sweet in a very sassy way."

"Oh, she is sassy alright. I have no clue how her husband can put up with her."

"You are just acting like a brother. I can see why he puts up with her. She is gorgeous."

"Whatever. You ready to go to the shooting range?"

"As ready as I will ever be," I say, feeling my stomach turn into knots.

CHAPTER 13

Sunny

We arrive at our destination. Looking to the right, I see the large sign that reads, "Honey Island Swamp Shooting Range." The logo alongside the sign is some type of creature that looks almost like a mossy big foot. I look over to Jackson with a questioning look while pointing to the sign.

"Okay, what is the animal on there? And please don't say it's a voodoo thing because I have had all the voodoo I can handle for one week."

"Ha, no, it's not voodoo. Legend has it there's a swamp monster out here. Same shit you hear across the country about bigfoot, but this one is a swamp monster."

He says this so nonchalantly while getting out of the Jeep. Before I take his hand to exit the car, I ask, "Well, is it for real?"

"Come on, Sunny, get out of the Jeep," he says, holding his hand out for me. His jaw tightens in annoyance with my question.

"What happened to you will have patience with me?" I ask.

"You're asking silly questions trying to avoid coming inside."

"No, I'm not. I just want to make sure I'm going to come out alive. Now is there a swamp thing in there or what?"

"Woman, you are testing my patience. No, there's no swamp thing. And if there is one, I will shoot it!"

"My hero," I say, taking his hand to step out of the Jeep.

We walk toward the structure, which appears to be a large patio nearby. Jackson has a big black bag swung over his back. The area appears deserted until a man pokes his head out of a little office at the end of the row.

"Hey, man, is that you, Jackson?"

"Yeah, it's me, old man," he yells back.

An older man maybe in his late sixties walks out. He's just as tall as Jackson and looks remarkably similar but with grey hair and a smaller muscle build. The man walks up to him as Jackson lets go of my hand wrapping him in a hug.

"Hey, Pops, sorry I haven't been here in a while. Been busy working."

Pops eyes me while Jackson is speaking. "Is it safe to say this pretty little thing works with you?"

"Watch your manners, Pops. This is Sunny, and yes, she's a friend and we work together."

"Hum, if you say so, Jackson." Pops holds his hand out to mine. I give it to him thinking he will shake it. "It's a pleasure to meet you, Miss Sunny, I'm Jackson's old man," he says as he kisses the top of my hand. "If my son doesn't treat you right, give me a call," he says playfully with a wink and a smile.

"Pops don't make me call Ma and have her come out here and whip your ass."

The older and still very handsome version of Jackson winks again at me as he walks back to his office and yells over his shoulder, "Pick a lane, son, any lane. You're the first person I've seen all day." With that, his father walks away and leaves us alone.

"Your dad is a sweet man."

"He's nothing but a dirty old man. My mom keeps his ass in check. He really means no harm."

"None taken. It's amazing how much all of you look alike."

"Who?"

"Who? You, your sister, and your dad."

"Enough gabbing, woman, let's get shooting."

Jackson puts his bag on the table and lays out all the guns, targets, and ammunition. I feel my blood pressure spike seeing the gun on the table. It brings me back to the clubhouse and how carelessly the guys would handle their guns, leaving them sitting out on the bar while they drank or on the table when they ate.

"I see I'm losing you, Sunny. Stay with me and listen to what I'm saying."

He goes on about the safety of the gun, how to load it, unload it, and what we are going to shoot at. He puts a piece of paper on a clip and hits the button, which sends it flying down the lane to the end of the row. Turning to me, he puts his hands on my shoulders, "I'm going to show you how to do it. Pay attention to my stance, and then you will shoot. Stay right here, and you'll be able to see me and stay in the safety zone."

He puts a pair of headphones for ear protection on my head, hands me safety glasses, and turns to the target. Everything about him is so sexy. I take him in slowly while he sets his stance. He has on a pair of jeans that should be illegal. They are hung low on his hips with the roundness of his perfect ass being hugged by the fabric. His black T-shirt hides nothing. It's a fitted shirt that highlights every muscle he has. His legs are spread wide and his muscular arms are extended. He is focused and serious as he eyes the target. The loud bang of the gun shakes me out of my ogling. He pulls the trigger over and over with the muscles in his arms and face flinching with each shot. It's so Goddamn hot to watch him, my fear of guns doesn't even register. Everything about him makes me feel safe yet I don't even know why. *"He's your tiger, Sunny,"* I hear the Voodoo Queen's voice in my head.

Jackson empties his gun, and then he presses the button to return his target. He grabs the paper and throws it on the table without inspecting it. I pick it up to check it out.

"Wow, every shot hit the two middle circles."

"Yeah, I haven't been here in a while. I need practice."

"Practice, I'm not sure I will be able to even hit the paper."

"Yes, you will."

"How do you know?" I say, stepping toward him and keeping eye contact. How can he be so confident? He has no clue how bad my aim is. As a kid, I could never hit any of the carnival targets—not in darts, toss games, shooting games, or balloon throwing.

"Follow my instructions and you will do it. Understand?"

I have to admit, I'm a bit intimidated now. There is not one ounce of play in him at the moment. *Get a grip on yourself. We are at a gun range, and this is no place for play.*

"Okay, I'm ready." I let out a loud breath.

"This is a Beretta Px4 Storm Subcompact. It's a perfect pocket pistol for a woman. It's small enough for you to fully control, and it can be set for single or double action trigger."

"Oh, I think single is all I can handle right now."

"Yeah, babe, you are correct. We're going to start on single, but you will finish with double when I'm done with you, along with your getting a concealed weapons permit. Put your safety glasses back on and stand where I was. I'm going to stand behind you and guide you. Let me do the work the first time so you can feel of the power."

"Okay," I whisper.

Feeling his heat behind me, I relax and let him take control. Who am I kidding? He has been in control from the moment I ran into him. He uses his foot to spread my legs to the desired shooting position. His feet are then placed on the outside of mine. His hard muscular body presses up against my back. His heat and manly scent is driving me crazy and my heart starts to race. I feel his grasp around my arm as he lifts it. His hot breath is in my ear. "Hold the gun, babe, but don't put your finger in the trigger yet, just hold it." I do as I'm told. He squats behind me for a moment eyeing up the target from my point of view.

"On the count of three, I'm going to pull the trigger, and we'll fire it ten times. Ready?"

I shake my head yes as words are not formable due to the sexual tension I'm feeling right now.

"One, two, three," he says, and the gun goes off. Bang, bang, bang, ten times. The vibration isn't as bad as I imagined with very little kick. I kept my eye on the target while I pulled the trigger. The gun stops and I don't move enjoying his body up against mine.

"You good, Sunny?"

"That was amazing. Can I try pulling the trigger alone?"

"That's what we're here for, babe," I hear as he steps away, and I feel the loss of his heat.

I turn in panic. "But I still need you to stand behind me. I'm not sure I'm that ready yet."

"Just stepping away to reload the gun, babe."

He loads the gun with a knowing grin on his face. "You will never have to beg me to be pressed up against your backside, Sunny."

We spend about an hour at the range. I am shocked at how fun and liberating it is. Jackson is patient and knowledgeable. I learned so much today. He has talked me into signing up for classes to get my concealed weapons permit. But before we leave, he makes me try one last round 'all alone!'

"You can do it, Sunny. I wouldn't allow you to do it if I didn't know you could do it. If you are going to carry a concealed weapon, you have to have confidence in your ability."

I take a deep breath knowing he's right, not only about the gun but also about my life. I have to be confident in my abilities, my strengths, and myself. I load the gun on my own and set my stance. Eyeing the target, I pull the trigger holding it in place and allowing it to unload the ten rounds.

I feel Jackson come up behind me hitting the button to return the target.

"Damn, girl, I better not piss you off," he says, holding the target up to me. All ten rounds made it in the middle three rings.

"I want to hit only the inner two rings next time," I say and pout.

"Getting a bit competitive, are we?"

"I like to win. Is that wrong?"

"No, not at all. Just don't expect to beat me at shooting, babe."

He closes the space between us wrapping his arms around my waist and looking down at me.

"You did an excellent job for a first-time shooter. Did you work up an appetite?"

"I did," I say, more breathless than intended.

"Seafood or burgers?" he asks, confusing me, as I did not have food on my mind at all.

"Oh, am I hungry? Yes, a little," I say, looking up into his glassy blue eyes.

"Yeah, you are going to test my patience, alright," he groans. "Let's get out of here and get some food," he says, smacking me hard on my ass.

Back in the city, we stop at a mom and pop shop that sells the most amazing fried seafood. We spend another hour or two just talking. I tell him about my dreams of going to college and becoming a nurse.

"Have you applied for grants yet?"

I chuckle thinking of how crazy things have been since I moved here. "I keep saying I have to do that but I have not."

"I can help you with that," he says sincerely.

"Oh yeah. Are you an expert at that or something?"

"Yeah, I guess you can say that. At the end of my military stint, I worked as a recruiter. Everyone gets the GI bill, but sometimes it's not enough, so I did a lot of research to help my guys find alternative ways to make their dreams happen. I'll look into grants for you and let you know what I find."

My heart swells with appreciation. I smile up at him. "Thank you, Jackson, that's really sweet of you to offer, and I have to admit, I have no clue what I'm doing so your advice is welcomed."

"Don't mention it, babe, I got this shit under control. We missed the spring registration, but we can get the paperwork going for the summer session. That will give you plenty of time to choose where you want to go and how we can get it paid for."

"Thank you," I tell him while trying not to let the tears of joy and appreciation run down my face. No one has ever cared enough about me to do this. I really shouldn't say that because my grandmother cared. She just didn't have the know-how to help me. I had decent grades in high school but nothing spectacular enough for the counselors to assume I wanted to go to college. I spent so much time taking care of the house, my grandmother, and trying to make extra money, I didn't have a ton of time to study like I should have.

I push away the negative thoughts of the past and toast to a new future with a large frozen margarita, and I allow myself to let my guard down. I want to let him into my world, drop the barriers, and let him know the real me.

Jackson is so handsome as he tells me about all the types of fish we can catch when we go fishing next weekend on his boat. I interrupt him when I just blurt out, "Rex was tracking me before I ran. He had a tracker the size of a pea sewed into every piece of clothing I owned." I keep my eyes focused on his. I don't know what came over me. I just felt the urge to give him the information he wanted from me. "I tried to run before I knew I was being tracked, and he and the entire damn Flaming Dragons came after me and took me from a gas station near Chicago. I went back with him because I only had two choices. Go back or die."

The anger that is stirred in Jackson's face is unmistakable. He gets up from his side of the booth and slides in next to me putting his strong arm around me and his other hand over mine.

"So how did you finally get away?" he asks softly.

I give him all the details about Joe and my escape. When I'm done telling him my story, I feel freed. I look up into his eyes to see if they are looking at me in a different light, but they're unreadable. He raises his hand to the waitress and asks for the bill, not saying another word to me. He pays the bill, grabs my hand, and leads me to the Jeep. I'm starting to feel a bit stupid for telling him the story. I should have known it would be a turn-off. Who wants someone as used as I am? I'm still deep in my self-pity when Jackson gets into the other side. I don't even realize he's there until his hand wraps around my neck pulling me to his lips. His kiss is hard, rushed, and out of control. I open my lips to let him in. His grasp gets tighter at the nape of my neck, and it feels as if he is trying to rein himself in. I raise my hand and put it through the back of his hair matching the force he's gripping mine with. In an instant, his lips are gone, and I release my grasp of his hair, but he has not released me. He gently but firmly pulls my head back to gain access to my neck, kissing and sucking down to my collarbone.

"You are so beautiful, Sunny. I will never allow anyone to hurt you like that again. Do you hear me? I promise you that."

I do my best to say yes with my eyes. My mind is so wrapped up in the feeling of his tongue on my neck, I can't speak. I reach over the seat, place my hand on his thigh, and brush against his cock causing him to moan into my mouth. He is fully erect and oh-so large. Deviating from my original plan, I start to rub my hand lightly up and down his long wide bulge and it pulses under my fingers. Jackson takes possession of my mouth again matching the rhythm of his tongue with that of my strokes on his hardness.

The kiss is intense and open to his soul. I have never felt the need for someone like I feel the need for Jackson right now. Almost as if he can read my mind, he stops kissing me. "Babe, if you don't stop rubbing me like that, I'm going to come in my pants. And I have not done that since I was twelve."

I smile up at him. "Then take me to your place, Jackson, I need you."

He groans against my lips and closes his eyes tight. "As much as I need to make love to you right this second, right here, you deserve better than that. When I enter you for the first time, I want you to know I'm with you because I can't stand to be without you. I want you to know you're with me because you can't be without me and not because you're running scared." He raises his eyebrows looking for confirmation from me that I understand him.

But I don't answer. I remove my hand from his lap and place both hands on his cheeks. "Could you be any more perfect?"

"You may want to get to know me before you say that, babe, I'm full of flaws."

"I haven't seen one yet."

"Let me take you home before you see one," he jokes with a drop-dead sexy grin and starts the Jeep.

I lie in my bed that night in sheer joy. Silently I thank Joe for bringing me here, and I thank God for putting Joe in my life. This is where I take control and live the life that was meant for me.

The next few weeks are filled with dancing at the club and hanging out with Jackson. I learn about his time in the Army. He was an Army Ranger and did undercover missions in Iraq. Day in and day out, it was his job to stealthily follow subjects around to see where they were hiding weapons, who they were associating with, and who was the next suicide bomber. No wonder I had no clue he was following us that night in the French Quarter. I would like to say I knew he was there, but honestly I didn't. My instincts told me I was being watched, but I dismissed it.

Today is our official second date on his boat. I'm not a tomboy and don't like to get my hands dirty which I assume is a bit difficult to not do when you're fishing with a man like Jackson.

Leaving the dock from Jackson's house, we only take a few minutes to get to his fishing spot. He took it slow unsure if I would get seasick, but I seemed to be fine so far.

"Woman, you are going to learn to bait your hook on your own or you don't fish," he fusses while I try to take in the scenery.

I cross my arms giving him a smirk. "This fishing thing was not my idea, remember?"

"Yeah, I remember. Now pick up the shrimp and put it on the hook."

"Nope."

"What do you mean, no?"

"What I mean is, I don't touch raw slimy things with my fingers." With my arms crossed, I'm determined not to touch that nasty thing. This was his ideal date not mine.

"Geez, woman, really?"

"Yes, really."

He bends down shuffling around his toolbox. "Here, put these on and bait your damn hook."

I look up to see a pair of gloves flying my way. "Jackson, why do you want me to do this so bad? I'm just fine watching you fish."

He gets up from his seat coming over to me and lowering down onto his knee so we're eye to eye.

"Because any woman of mine will not be afraid to shoot a gun or bait a hook. That's why."

I just smile. Jackson Devereaux just called me his woman. I pull him into a kiss before he can get away. It's soft and unhurried. I want to take in this moment and etch it in my memory. Jackson just called me his woman. I pull away and rest my forehead onto his.

"Okay, if I have to bait the hook with gloves for you, then I will." He smiles back up at me.

"About Goddamn time," he says with a chuckle. "Now catch some fish so I can cook you a romantic dinner for the rest of our date tonight."

"The rest of our date? You didn't tell me we had more to this date. I don't have any clothes for a date."

"Don't stress. It's just us at my place."

I look at him with large eyes. Does he think he is going to cook me a romantic dinner while I will be in sweats? "If you're cooking me a romantic dinner, I need a romantic outfit."

He puts his head in his hands sighing out loud, "Okay, you can use my Jeep to go home and change while I cook. But fish right now or we won't have anything to eat."

I smile with a look of victory. Taking in the beautiful scenery around us, I bait the hook like a pro and throw my line in the water. There are beautiful large cypress trees with their knees poking out of the water. Turtles go by the boat as we sit in happy silence fishing. I watch Jackson fish, and I pretty much just sit and hold the pole. It's now late January and we are in the middle of a warm spell. Jackson has on a long-sleeved shirt but it is so snug I can see his muscles flex as he reels in his fish. He's so handsome I have to pinch myself to see if I'm really sitting here with him, as his "woman." Oh, how I need to be with him tonight. I have the perfect dress picked out for seduction tonight.

The fishing trip ends after Jackson has caught five large red fish, and it's time for us to head back. When he helps me out of the boat, my hand courses with the continued electricity I feel every time he touches me; it's unbearable and I need him. I know he is trying to be romantic, but I want to throw him down on the lawn and demand he takes me now. My nightmares of Rex have been replaced with fantasies of Jackson. Since the shooting range, I wake most mornings soaking wet and sexually frustrated. Sometimes I'm so cranky in the mornings I have to touch myself to release the pressure. So there I lie morning after morning wet for Jackson and extending my dreams by feeling my own wetness. I imagine my finger circling my clit is his tongue, and when I plunge two fingers deep within myself, I wish it was his hard cock. When I pump my fingers in and out with my wetness dripping, visions of Jackson dance in my head. I come but am never fully relieved of the sexual tension I hold for him. I don't want to do that anymore, I can't. It's getting harder and harder to get myself off without being able to touch him.

"Sunny," I hear as I shake my head trying to bring myself out of my daydream.

"Earth to Sunny. Are you there?"

"I'm sorry. I was daydreaming."

He pulls me into a hug standing out on the dock. "What are you daydreaming about with that big smile of yours?"

I reach up on my toes giving him a quick peck on the lips. "You'll find out later. Now where are your keys? I have to go get all dolled up for our romantic date."

He reaches into his pocket and pulls out his keys. "Be back at 7:00 p.m. on the dot. I have my own surprise and I don't want wait."

"I can't wait to see what you have planned. I will be here at 7:00 p.m. on the dot." He kisses my forehead and I'm off to get ready.

CHAPTER 14

Sunny

Entering the apartment, I see Carmella walking around only wrapped in a towel and moping.

"What's the matter?" I ask, shutting the door behind me.

She looks up at me in surprise. "Oh shit, you scared me, girl. I didn't expect you back so soon."

"Yeah, well, Jackson has a date planned for us at his house, and I wanted to wear something nice. Crazy man thought we could go fishing then have a romantic dinner in this." I wave my hands up and down my body.

She looks up at me in shock. "He planned a romantic dinner for you?"

"Yes, surprising, huh?"

"You can say that again. Can he cook?"

"I know he can make a mean breakfast. I will let you know tomorrow if he can cook dinner. So where are you getting ready to go?"

"Dinner with Kevin."

"Then what's up with the sorry for myself look you have going on?"

"I'm just not sure he's the guy for me. He's too boring for me."

"Boring? I thought you said he had his penis pierced."

"Yeah, that's how he lured me in, but that is the height of his excitement. He's a fuck buddy, not someone I want to have conversation with and pretend I like."

"I'm sorry, Carmella. So why are you going out with him if you don't like him?"

"Duh, the penis piercing. I can't say goodbye to it yet. So I'll try to make it through the dull dinner and fuck him as soon as I can," she laughs.

"You are bad, do you know that?"

"Yes, I do and I love it. So what are you gonna wear for your big sexy night tonight? And please tell me you are going to make that man take care of you. I'm sick of hearing you make yourself happy every morning."

My face turns beet red as I gasp and cover my mouth with my hand. "Carmella!"

"What? This is a small apartment. I hear everything. Don't be embarrassed. We are both adults, remember? That is the exact reason I'm still with Mr. Dick Piercing so I don't have to do myself every morning like you do. Now enough about me. Let's pick out something for you to wear. Something he can't resist."

We walk to her closet, and I can't do anything but shake my head at her bluntness. She is right though. When we reach her closet, she starts to clap. "I have the perfect dress for you." She pulls out a ruby red dress. "This will look great on you."

This dress is a little satin thing that could be confused as lingerie. The top is a halter-top with a deep plunging neckline that is almost to my waist. The back plunges all the way down to the crack of my rear with a satin belt that ties the dress on. It's plain yet dressy due to its shimmer and shine. While it's a full-length dress that hits the floor, I would've never thought to wear it in public. Since our dinner is in the privacy of Jackson's home, it's perfect. I look up at Carmella as she is waiting for a response.

"Do you like it?"

"I love it, but do you have a full-length coat I can wear over it to get to the car? I don't think I should walk to my car in the middle of the French Quarter dressed like this."

She is so easily excited, she bounces up and down clapping her hands. "I have the perfect stripper jacket, no pun intended."

I just shake my head at her and smile. "None taken, my friend. Now let me get into the shower so I have time for painting my nails."

She smacks my ass on the way out of the room, and I'm not the least bit surprised by her show of affection. It's so Carmella.

I spend the next two hours showering, exfoliating, shaving, painting my fingernails and toe nails, putting on my going out face, and pulling my hair into a very sleek up-do. Finally, it's time to put the dress on. I pull the dress over my head letting the soft fabric skim my naked body. Oh, the silk feels amazing, and with my heightened senses, my nipples pucker through the fabric. This dress leaves no room for a bra; however, I pull on a thong in an attempt not to have a wet spot on the back of the dress. I'm so turned on right now at the thought of being with Jackson that the slightest touch will send me into an orgasm.

I look into the mirror at my reflection, and I have to admit, this dress is hot. I put on my grandmother's heart locket thinking of how far I have come. She would be proud to see me break away from the devil. I let the cold metal fall to my neck while slipping on my sky-high red heels before walking out to find Carmella waiting on the sofa.

Her jaw drops and she just stares. "I knew you were hot, girl, but this is off the charts. If I went both ways, I would so do you."

Again, I shake my head at her as she stands and gives me a hug. "You are smoking hot. Give him hell, girl, and don't come home tonight."

"I 'll do my best to."

"Oh, trust me, I doubt you will even get to the first course dressed like that." She kisses my cheek and hands me her long black jacket. I pull it on and head out to Jackson's with twenty-five minutes to spare.

On the way over to Jackson's, I start to get a nervous feeling. With the feeling of being watched, I keep looking into the rear view mirror to make sure there's no one in the back seat or following me. *What the hell is wrong with you? No one is there and no one is following you. Don't ruin this night.*

Once I press my fears down, I start to hear the Voodoo Queen's voice in my head. *"Trust your instincts. Don't let your guard down."*

"Crazy freaking woman, what the hell does she know?" I say out loud. I turn the radio up to drown out the sounds of my mind. Within no time, I pull up at Jackson's. It's dark out when I pull up. My heart skips with panic and lust. I jump out and hustle to the door not wanting to be outside alone too long. Reaching for the doorknob, I don't bother to knock and just walk in.

"I hope you don't mind, I let myself in," I say, looking around for Jackson. The house smells amazing, and it looks beautiful with the dancing light of all the candles he has placed all over the room. I hear low music playing in the background while I walk closer to the beautifully lit table. My mind starts to work over time again, and I hear the Voodoo Queen's voice again. *"Lock the door, my child."*

I huff and turn to lock the door, not sure why I'm listening to the crazy voices in my head. Before I can turn around, I feel a hand pull me back until my back is flush with a rock hard chest. A brief moment of fear took over, but it is quickly washed away when I smell Jackson's scent.

"You're five minutes early. In a hurry for something, babe?"

I turn into his arms and look up at his beautiful face. For a handsome man, his face is just so beautiful. His eyes slowly move to my lips. "Those lips, woman, are gonna kill me, they look so wet and hot."

I swipe my tongue out slowly over my lips to draw him in.

"Fuck, I want to kiss them, but I don't want to mess them up," he says, lifting his hand to my face.

"They're kissable so please kiss them." He does as he is told pulling my face to his and kissing me senseless at the door.

He pulls away slowly. "Let me take your coat. Did it get cold outside?" He gives me a curious look wondering why I have this heavy coat on. Pulling the coat down my arms slowly, he answers his own question. He stands in awe staring at me with fire in his eyes. They start at my barely covered breasts, which are only covered by the thin satin fabric coming down from my halter-top. I feel my nipples harden under his hot gaze.

"Are you going to stand there and stare all night or you going to feed me?" I ask, wanting to have our romantic dinner.

He throws my coat over the sofa. "You may have to put the coat back on in order to get through dinner. Turn around. Let me see all of you."

I obey without question turning around and keeping my eyes on his. The back of the dress is low enough to show the horrible tattoo, but I had Carmella touch it up quickly. It's almost gone so not much was needed; I only have two treatments left.

"Let's eat," he demands. "If I touch you now, we will never make it to the table, and I have slaved over the stove for two hours making the perfect meal for the perfect woman."

I look over to where he has the table set, and it is absolutely the most romantic thing I've ever seen. The table is set for two with long tapered candles lit surrounded by little candles scattered around the room. There's a fresh bouquet of flowers in the center. Yep, you heard that correctly. The big hunk of muscle has flowers set out on the table. I see a bottle of wine chilling in a bucket with two glasses waiting for us. The curtains are drawn and everything looks like a scene from a movie.

"Are you ready to eat, babe?" Jackson asks, holding his hand out to me. I shake my head and take his hand allowing him to lead the way. His left hand settles on the nakedness of my back stirring the existing heat I have rising in my body. Reaching the table, he pulls the chair out for me, and I sit in amazement of his lovely creation. Once I'm seated, his hand lightly runs over my shoulders spreading chills over my heated skin.

He returns with a large bowl filled with salad in one hand and a small basket of bread in the other.

"You made salad and bread?" I ask in surprise.

"I warmed rolls and mixed a salad. I can cook, babe, but making bread is something I don't do," he chuckles. Setting the bowls down, he motions for me to fill my plate as he pours white wine. After our salad, he presents the dish that is responsible for the wonderful smell, Crawfish Monica pasta! It's rotini pasta covered in a spicy cream sauce mixed with crawfish.

"Absolutely amazing," I moan after my first bite. "Where did you learn to cook?"

"My mom. She taught Melinda and I both how to at a young age. Once she had to go down to the bayou to take care of my dying grandmother for a few weeks, and my dad could barely function without her. He fed us boxed food and take-out for three full weeks. He couldn't cook, clean, or do laundry. When we ran out of clothes, he took us to the store and bought new ones." He smiles as he relives his childhood memory.

"He didn't know how to turn on the wash machine?"

"I'm sure he could've figured it out if he wanted to, but he is from *that era*"—he makes air quotes—"You know, the southern era where the woman does all so he simply refused."

"Thank goodness, your mom came back," I laugh.

"Yeah, she was so pissed when she came home. The house was a disaster. I think Melinda and I were about eight years old and Mom had done everything so we didn't know what to do. From that day on, she taught both of us how to do it all. Her life became easier and we learned how to take care of ourselves never having to depend on others to do for us."

"She sounds like an amazing woman."

"That she is. Anyone that has been married to my dad for fifty years is more than amazing," he laughs. "I mean really, you met my dad. He is a crazy old guy."

"He was sweet."

"So are you ready for dessert?" he says, wanting to get this dinner over with.

"Oh, I don't know if I can fit any more," I say, patting my belly.

"Don't give me that crap, woman. You're skinny enough for one small piece of cheesecake."

"Cheesecake, that's my favorite dessert."

"Then you'll have a piece."

Jackson gets up again to retrieve the dessert. While he's away, I hear the radio change stations and now playing slow country music. When he returns to the table, I take a moment for the first time tonight to take in his attire. I had arrived a few minutes early, and I'm guessing he was not fully dressed yet. He has on a casual white dress shirt with some tan linen pants that are so sexy hanging low on his hips. I can't help but think just one pull of that string around his waist ...

"Sunshine, I lost you again." I hear his deep voice breaking me out of my sexy vision. "Would you like more wine with your cheesecake?"

"Yes, please." I blush, knowing he caught me gawking.

"Where do you go when you zone out like that?"

I look up at him in embarrassment. Should I really tell him where my mind was?

"Nowhere in particular. Just deep in thought, that's all."

He puts a forkful of cheesecake in his mouth giving me a knowing grin. "You do know you will tell me where that dirty mind of yours was before the night is over?"

"Oh, you think so?"

"Yeah, I think I'll be able to drag it out of you."

"And how do you suppose you'll do that?"

He stands and walks over to me with hypnotic eyes. "Let's dance, Sunny. I need to get my hands on that hot as hell dress before I rip it off."

I take a purposefully long sip of my wine before taking his hand. He walks me over to the middle of the living room, which is just as equally romantically lit as the dining room. He pulls me close with that burning hot hand still on my back. I allow myself to let go and let this relationship blossom. We start to sway along to the music and it feels effortless to be in his arms without fear. Jackson dips his head placing his lips on my neck and slowly kissing it. The soft slow kisses mixed with his hot breath causes an involuntary shiver. I've never wanted a man this badly. I slide my hands under his shirt gliding them over his bare back and run them over his muscles. I feel his back tighten under my touch. I smile at the thought of him holding back trying to take it slow.

We don't stop swaying allowing our hands to roam over each other's bodies. His large hands have danced their way down to my ass grasping it with need. I feel the same need and desire in my core. My nipples are as hard as diamonds from the friction of the satin and the pressure of being pressed up against Jackson's hard chest. I want him now. I don't want him to hold back. I don't want him to treat me like a wounded animal.

I whisper in his ear, "Want to know where my mind was earlier?"

"Yes," he says with a hoarse voice.

"I was wondering what I would find when I pulled that neatly tied string around your waist."

He chuckles, "Are you sure you're ready?"

"I'm more ready than I've ever been in my life. Please don't treat me like a porcelain doll due to my past."

He looks down at me and into my eyes. "I won't. You're mine and your past is gone."

I raise my hands snaking them around his neck and pulling his lips to mine and take his mouth with force and want. The passion that pours out of me is unrecognizable. I had never been this sexual before. Yeah, sex was okay, but I was never the one that had to have it. And here I am demanding it from this perfect male specimen.

He pulls away from me with determination. "I have seen almost everything you own at the strip club but never could I have imagined I would have you in my arms like this."

"Now that you have me, what are you going to do with me?" I ask breathlessly.

"Never let you go."

I sigh as he takes his turn at being in control of our kiss. At first, it's soft and sweet but quickly gets out of control in a good way. His hands are all over me, and I quiver under his fingers. Oh, those fingers are like magic. With a simple snap, he unbuttons my dress allowing it to fall to my waist and expose my breasts to him. He has seen them before as we dance topless, but most dances require tassels to cover our nipples. He looks down at my full breasts and cups them in his hands like a prized possession. Bending his head, he takes one nipple into his mouth gently sucking while he rolls the other between his fingertips. The light touch of his tongue on one with the tight, hard rolling pressure of the other is beyond amazing. Amazing is such a poor description of what he's making me feel. I throw my head back and let the pleasure take over.

"Oh, Jackson," I gasp in shock at the reality that I'm about to come. This man is making me have an orgasm, and he hasn't even touched my pussy yet. I put my fingers in his hair pulling him closer to me trying to get more. I'm on the brink of ecstasy. His suction increases pulling my nipple in with his teeth sending a flash of pain followed by exquisite pleasure. That's when I see stars, and my body trembles while I call out his name. He continues to lick and roll my nipples gently until my body stills, and then he pulls me into an intense embrace.

"That has never happened to me before," I whisper. "What are you doing to me, Jackson?" I grin up at him.

"About to make love to you," he says, pulling the belt around my waist releasing my dress. It slides down my newly shaven legs pooling at my feet. "If that is a new feeling to you, I have a lot of catching up to do, babe."

"You will have to wait your turn for show and tell, handsome." Dropping to my knees, I pull the string on his pants releasing them to find their place in a pool across from my dress. My eyes have to be as big as saucers right now. First of all, he is commando, yep, nothing under those sexy pants of his but his pure hot muscles of steel. Secondly and most importantly, I'm taken by his size. He's a very large man standing at 6'3" with the most beautiful penis I have ever seen. I know, ladies, they're not really pretty, but you haven't seen this one. It's long and thick with a perfectly round head. I stare at it in amazement watching it jerk under my gaze.

"You're killing me up here. Snap out of the daydream, darling."

I look up at him from under my eyelashes slowly taking him into my mouth and placing one hand at his shaft not sure I'll be able to take all of him. But I'm sure as hell going to try. I hear him groan as I open a little wider to let him go deeper working his shaft with my other hand. I slowly pull away licking his slit gently while massaging his balls.

"Fuck, Sunny, you have to slow down or I'm gonna lose my shit here."

I ignore his plea taking him in again and sucking hard while pulling away. The sense of power I feel right now is so exhilarating, I feel the wetness increasing. When I feel his balls tighten, I know I'm almost home free. But before I take him down again, his large arms are under mine pulling me into his. I wrap my legs around his waist pressing my heels into his firm ass while he walks to the sofa.

"I can't wait another damn minute, Sunny, I need to be inside of you like yesterday."

"Then what are you waiting for? Jackson, I'm so wet for you."

He lays me over the arm of the sofa with my ass propped up and my back lying across the cushions. He kneels in front of me pulling my thong down in one slow sultry motion.

"Do you know how beautiful your pussy is, Sunny?"

"As beautiful as your enormous cock?" I reply.

"You and that dirty mouth. It's going to get you in trouble, do you know that?"

"I sure hope so." I smirk.

Without another word, he licks me from the bottom entrance up to my clit. His tongue is stiff and wide as it passes smoothly up my slick channel. He slowly rubs circles around my entrance with his fingers as he batters my clit with the same hard motions of his tongue. I feel the tingling of another orgasm building once again in my core. He quickly shoves two fingers inside of me. I see fireworks as he picks up the speed and intensity pushing me over my peak. He waits for my breathing to slow while gently lapping at my pussy.

I hear him fumbling in his pants followed by the unmistakable sound of a condom being ripped open. Just the sound of it brings me to the edge. My body is on fire like never before.

I don't have the ability to lift my head yet as the second orgasm was more intense then the first. I have never come twice during sex ever, and we haven't even gotten to the sex yet.

"Look at me, Sunny. I want you here with me and out

of your daydream when I take you. You hear me, Sunny, look at me."

I look up at him with sweat glistening over his body reflecting in the candlelight as if he is glowing. Usually my eyes are closed with my head and mind elsewhere during sex, but not with Jackson. My heart stops as I gaze up at him with the feeling of love I have for him. Am I falling for him? Yes, I'm falling in love with Jackson Devereaux.

"You with me, babe?"

"I'm with you," I say, looking down at his beautiful cock. The muscles in his arm roll as he uses his hand to direct his cock up and down my soaking wet slit.

"You make me so fucking hard, Sunny. I have never wanted someone so much. I love the way you respond to my touch."

"I can't take it anymore, Jackson, please fuck me, Jackson, I need ..."

He slams into me with such force I don't finish my sentence. He strokes in and out of me asking, "What do you need, Sunny? Tell me what you need, and I will give it to you."

"I need it harder, Jackson."

He growls deep as he drives his cock balls deep into my core. He's fucking me hard but slow and the feeling is to die for. Due to his size and the position of my ass being hiked up on the sofa, he is so deep. I moan in pleasure as the scent of us mixed together consumes me.

"Oh, Sunny, you're so tight. You feel so good wrapped around me."

He picks up the pace while lifting my ass with both his hands. I thought he was as deep as he could go a minute ago, but at this angle, he is so deep, I don't think he can go any deeper. As he loses control and fucks me wildly, angels start to sing and I come with such force I don't recognize my own voice while I scream out his name. My scream pushes him over the edge and we come together. I clamp down on him while he's still pulsing inside of me.

"You keep doing that and I won't be able to stop fucking you tonight."

"That's the plan, babe."

He bends down, lifts me off the sofa, and carries me to his bed. Putting me down in the middle, he says, "Don't move. I'll be right back."

As if I were going anywhere. Just as that thought crosses my mind, I hear the flicker of a lighter and the room comes alive. I'm in the middle of his king-sized four-poster mahogany bed. The more candles he lights, the more I can see. I've been in his bed before, but I was too busy looking at the pictures to notice the bed. How did I miss it? It's massive. He kisses my head and walks away from me to the bathroom. I watch him walk away and ogle his perfect ass not believing this man is mine.

I take my heels off and slip under the covers feeling chilly from the loss of his body heat. I snuggle under his comforter wrapping my arms around myself trying to replace his heat. When my fingers run over my skin, the need to touch myself is overwhelming. How can I want more? This man has made me come three times and my body is still wanting more.

I decide to take part in the new sexual me. Jackson brought it out in me and now I can't stop it. I let my fingers lightly skim my nipples as my other hand grazes my pussy lips. The feeling is no match to what Jackson did to me but I need it. I hear the door open but I don't stop. He stands at the side of the bed in his full naked glory only heightening my need and the pace of my fingers.

"Woman, what are you doing to me?" he asks as his cock starts to come back alive.

He looks at me knowing exactly what I'm doing, and his dick continues to respond. I pull the covers off myself allowing him to watch. I have never even opened my eyes in private to watch myself do this, much less let someone else watch me. But it feels erotic and natural with him.

"What are you doing to me is the real question?" I ask while rolling my nipple and sliding my finger up and down my slit. "I have never felt like this before, Jackson. I have never had three orgasms, much less three and wanting, no needing, more."

He starts to stroke himself as he watches and listens to me. He is such a magnificent sight. I watch as the muscles in his arms flex with each stroke. His cock growing larger makes me feel more erotic and in control.

"Make yourself come for me, Sunny."

His request turns the heat up within my core as I let my middle finger dive into my pussy while my thumb circles my clit. The look of desire in his eyes is so pure. My other hand is twisting and turning my nipple with such pain it creates a pleasure that's unreal.

"Go ahead, do it, Sunny, come for me."

On cue, the sensation hits me. I rock my hips up to meet the force of my hand as my nipple feels the biting pressure of my fingers. I close my eyes tight letting the feeling take over my body only slowing once I have ridden out the entire orgasm. I was so taken over by the feeling I didn't feel him get into the bed. I pull my finger out of myself only to have it captured by Jackson's mouth.

"Do you know how good your pussy tastes, Sunny?"

I smile at him. "You like it?"

"I love it. That was so fucking hot that I'm hard as a rock again. Do you know how physically impossible this is?"

"Considering I've never in my life come this much in one day, much less during one sexual experience, yes, I understand how impossible it is."

He leans over kissing the side of my neck and whispering in my ear, "I will never let you go. You're mine." He lifts my hand placing my fingers back into my entrance and slowly moving them in and out a few times. I moan in pleasure then in anger as he pulls them out.

"What are you doing? I was enjoying that," I giggle.

"I know, and I want you to taste how much you enjoy that."

He lifts my fingers to my lips. I open them letting him slide my fingers in. I close my lips around my fingers sucking them and tasting my own juices as he pulls my fingers out of my mouth.

"Is that good?" he asks.

"It's sexy," I say, looking back at him for more.

"You're Goddamn right, that's sexy. I need you one more time."

He flips me over in one swoop pulling me up onto my knees.

"You like it from behind?"

I shrug my shoulders not sure how to answer the question. I didn't really like it this way, but I really never wanted to have sex with a man the way I want Jackson. "Not sure," I say, looking back at him.

He smiles and slams into my wet channel hard and fast. I didn't even notice he had put on a condom, but I can feel he has one on. *Mental note: get on the pill.* My side conversation doesn't last long as I'm pulled away by his fingers rubbing circles on my clit as he strokes in and out of me slowly with his rock hard cock. I brace my arms on the mattress and rock back and forth to meet his thrusts feeling myself getting wetter each time I push back on him harder.

"You're going to fucking kill me, woman, you feel so good," he groans. When he starts to peak, he clamps down hard on my clit squeezing and pulling while pumping in and out of me. I feel another orgasm approach, and pulling on my own nipples, I explode in a million pieces. We both collapse in exhaustion, and I'm down for the count. My body is like jello with the aftereffect of my orgasm still pulsing through me from my head to my toes.

Moments later, Jackson lifts his weight off me and

mumbles something about picking up the kitchen and blowing out candles. I'm absolutely exhausted, yet I can't seem to fall asleep without him.

Quicker than I expected, he's back in the bed pulling me to him and wrapping those wonderfully strong arms around me. Every inch of my naked back is flush with his and it's such a glorious feeling. Wrapped in my cocoon of Jackson, I feel my self starting to drift off into happiness.

CHAPTER 15

Sunny

The next few weeks fly by as I'm wrapped in a whirlwind of emotions. I try to fight the feeling of falling too fast. My brain is telling me to put a wall up, to take it slower. But my heart has me jumping in feet first with no life preserver. Jackson and I are typically on the same work schedule, which has given us a lot of time together. Most of our off time is spent in his bed, on the kitchen table, in his boat, and just about anywhere we are left alone. Every fiber of my being is drawn to him.

It's a slow Wednesday at the club. Tuesdays and Wednesdays are the worst two days of the week to work, and as expected, it's slow as molasses tonight. There aren't many people in the club and fewer people in the exotic room, which is where I'm scheduled tonight. Jackson has made sure he's not working the exotic room while I perform since we have been together. I don't think he can take the fact that my body is being bared to other men now that he's taken claim. And to be honest, I'm over it as well. Summer can't come fast enough. I'm ready to leave this world behind me and become a student.

"Hey, Ms. Daydreamer," I hear someone say. I shake my head to pull myself out of my daydream to notice Carmella standing there.

"Girl, your name needs to be changed to Ms. Daydreamer because that is all your ass does lately. I mean really, are you not with that hunk of muscles enough that you have to drool over him every second you are not with him?"

I laugh, "Don't hate because you had to dump Mr. Dick Piercing."

"Oh, you're wrong for that," she mutters, throwing me my pom-poms, hitting me in the face while I continue to laugh at her. "Now get your pigtails and cheerleading ass on that stage and empty their pockets." She smiles at me.

I run on stage to start my schoolgirl cheerleading skit. My auburn hair is pulled into two high pigtails on each side of my head. I have on the cutest red and white cheerleading outfit ever. I may have to slip this in my bag tonight for a special Jackson performance. The music starts and my body moves to the music, mostly to an empty room. I zone out seeing images of Jackson and I together to push me through the routine. Being the daydreamer I am, I do get a bit lost in my own thoughts forgetting I'm on stage. A mental filmstrip of Jackson plays in my mind, and I'm interrupted by a strange voice calling my name. As I look up, my heart stops and my hands start to shake. I see a man covered in tattoos with a black cut on. The cut alone has my entire body trembling inside with fear. *Has he found me?* Just as the thought crosses my mind, he turns to his buddy laughing, and I get a view of his patch. *Thank you, Jesus.* It's not a Flaming Dragon patch. His cut says Bayou Bandits.

I take a deep breath and continue to move while my shaking subsides. Just as I have myself under control, he gets up from his chair throwing a $100 bill at my feet with a grin. "That was the best damn dance I've seen, sugar. You want to give me and my boys a private dance?" Grinning wide he shows his broken teeth.

Before I can respond, Parke has stepped between the biker guy and the stage cutting off the man's view of me.

"Sunny doesn't do private dances," Parke growls without budging and standing tall with his large muscular frame.

The other men from the biker's table stand ready to

defend him. But the biker guy puts his hands up. "Hey, sorry, I just had to check. How about a lap dance, your girls do lap dances don't they?" he asks, looking around Parke to me.

Parke does not have to turn to me for an answer. He knows I've never done lap dances before, and I most certainly don't do them now. The song is over, and I pick up tips from the floor and walk quickly back stage letting Parke handle the biker. Once I'm backstage, the emotions of seeing the biker and thinking Rex could have found me hits me hard. With my back to the wall, I lose it. Sliding down the wall to the floor, I sit and sob. The realization that he may find me one day causes my body to involuntarily shiver.

Carmella rushes in and finds me on the floor. "What the fuck was that about? What did he do to you, are you okay?"

I look up at her with dazed eyes. "That could have been him. And just like you always say, I'm out there daydreaming about Jackson and had no clue a table full of bikers was there the entire time sitting in front of my face."

"Shhh, honey, you are going to be fine. Jackson would not let anyone hurt one hair on that beautiful head of yours."

"You have no idea how viscous Rex can be."

"Are you saying Mr. Muscles can't handle him?"

"No, what I am saying is, I can't keep going up there and zoning out. I have to be alert."

"Well, duh, I've been telling you that since you started."

I wipe the tears from my face and give her a small grin because as usual she's right. "But what am I going to do? I suck at dancing when I'm not zoned out."

"You are gonna have to figure a way for the next few months. Come on, we're already halfway through February, and you're quitting at the end of May. You need to save the money so you won't have to work here while you're in school."

"I know, you're right. I will figure it out." She pulls me up and off the ground into a tight hug.

"Bitch, you need to get your shit together because you're always making me mushy and shit," she says, playfully pushing me toward the dressing room. As I change, she stays with me knowing I'm still a little shaken.

"Hey, I have some tequila out here when you get dressed. We need to shake this shit off. We need to get your mind off this. How about we hit the parades on Sunday? You're off Sunday right?"

"Yeah, I'm off but I don't know. I've never been to a parade before, and I show enough boobs here. I don't really want to flash for free."

"Oh my gawd! I hate tourists. Don't be a tourist. We don't flash for beads. Only tourists do that. And it's not about catching the beads. It's just a fun experience. If you have never been, I'm not taking no for an answer. We're going. Jackson can come along, and we'll see if Samantha and Parke want to come as well."

I step out of the dressing room ready for my shot. "When do you think the two of them will admit they have something going on?"

"Hopefully soon because the sexual tension in the air between them drives me nuts."

We both laugh and down our shots.

"Okay, I'm in. We will go to the parade."

"That's my girl."

Samantha

"Wednesdays suck!" I say out loud to no one. The club is half-empty with only a handful of men in the exotic room and the sex room literally has four people in there. I put my head in my hands trying to figure out what to do. While the club is making money as a whole, it is costing me more money to pay my employees on Tuesdays and Wednesdays than it brings in on those two days.

My office door opens, and I look up from my hands to see problem number two. Or I should say problem number one, as Parke has become something I can't ignore for much longer. He has been chipping away at my wall since day one, and the bricks are about to crumble. I can feel it.

"Yes, Parke, is there a problem?"

"It looks like I should be asking you that. You okay?"

I wave my hand at him to have him shut the door. I don't want everyone knowing I'm thinking about closing the club on Tuesdays and Wednesdays yet.

"I'm fine but I'm debating on closing the club on the two slow days. What do you think?"

"Thank fuck," he grunts.

I look up at him in surprise. "You have an issue with working the two slow days?"

"No, but it doesn't take a genius to figure out there are more employees than customers on most slow days. That causes a problem out there for security. When the customers feel like they own the place, they get unruly and crude. I just had to throw out five Bayou Bandits. They demanded a private party with Sunny."

"Shit, is she okay?"

"Well, of course, she's okay. Why wouldn't she be? The stage dancers have security on them at all times while dancing."

I look up at him and shake my head in confirmation. *Damn it. That had to scare her. Parke doesn't know her past with bikers and it's not his business.*

"Yeah, you're right, Parke. Sorry, I'm not thinking straight. I know you all have it under control. It's just I'm sure she's not used to bikers, that's all."

"I think closing on the two slow days would be good for everyone. The girls don't like working them anyway."

"Really?"

"Really, Samantha. You need to pay attention to the girls and get your head out of the sex room."

I snap my head toward him with a fierce look. "What the hell is that supposed to mean?"

"Nothing. Let me know what you decide. I have work to do," he groans, turning to walk away.

Who in the hell does he think he is? I grab him by the arm before he reaches the door. "I don't think so, Parke. You need to explain yourself."

"You're so consumed with making sure the sex room stays going, you don't pay attention to the girls. They're your bread and butter to keeping this club going. Why are you so involved in the sex room? It runs itself. You have members lined up for a year to get in there."

"What do you mean, why am I so involved? I'm the fucking owner in case you haven't noticed."

"Oh, I noticed. Trust me, I know you're the boss every fucking day," he says, moving closer to me. I back up until I'm flush against the wall. His face is so close to mine.

"You know what I think, Samantha? I think you hide up in that room because you're hiding from me. I think you want me more than you're willing to admit."

The rage I feel stirring within me is uncontrollable. How dare he call me out. My hand goes up without a thought and lands right across his cheek. I'm not sure if it was the force or the surprise that turns his head. I regret it immediately but it's done. When he turns his head back to me slowly, I see the son of a bitch is smiling at me. It's the sexiest fucking smile I've seen on his face. I wait for his response but the words don't come. His lips slam onto mine followed with his body. His hand grips the nape of my neck with his fingers entwined in my hair keeping my head in place and giving him access to my mouth. I fight him for a millisecond before I give in and kiss him back.

My mind is racing. *I have to stop this. My rule, I can't be with him. Oh, fuck that rule.* He pushes me up against the wall with all his weight pressing his hard cock into me. He slows the pace of his kiss, opening his eyes and looking at me with hunger. Removing his lips from mine, he says, "You have two options, Samantha. Throw your rule out the fucking window or fire me. Either way, I'm going to fuck you on that desk. So think quick."

"I threw the rule out the window the second I slapped you," I say with a smile.

A broad smile crosses his face, and I feel his hand on my ass picking me up. I wrap my legs around his waist as he walks over to the door to lock it, carrying me as if I weigh nothing. He strides back to my desk, leans over, swipes everything there to the ground, and lays me down on my back. My body is on fire for him. Feeling the loss of his heat, I reach up pulling his tie and bringing him back down to me with my legs pulling his cock to my core. We're both fully dressed but you wouldn't know it by the panting sounds echoing off the walls.

I put my finger in the knot of his tie and untie it while he devours my mouth. He hovers over me while I unbutton his shirt needing to feel his heated skin against mine. I knew he was fit, but I was taken aback by how fit he really is. This man does not have a six-pack; I think he is carrying an entire fucking case. I push his shirt over his wide shoulders getting a full glimpse of his true glory. I let out a breathy moan gliding my hands over his chest and skimming his nipples.

In a slow dramatic motion, Parke pulls the tie at my waist releasing my knit dress and giving him a view of what's underneath. Let's just say, I believe in very sexy undergarments at all times. I mean really y'all, I run a sex club. What else did you expect?

Parke's eyes light up like a six-year-old on Christmas

morning when he pulls my dress open and exposes my all-black ensemble. This sexy number was not cheap and it's paying me back in dividends. He rubs his hands over the black lace garter belt that holds my ultra-silky thigh highs up. As he wraps his hand around my waist, his fingers sketch a path over my ass as if he is ensuring my panties are indeed a thong.

"Jesus, woman, I knew you were hot as hell," he says and pauses, looking at my satin bra that has my breasts pushed up looking amazing. "But reality has nothing on my imagination."

"Ditto," I say, pulling him back to me and wanting his mouth on mine. But he doesn't take my mouth. His lips skim over my neck sucking and licking down to my collarbone then to my breasts. His large hands cup my breasts with his thumbs rubbing over my nipples through the expensive silk fabric making my core clench with wetness. He pulls the fabric down taking one nipple in his mouth, sucking with sweet soft pressure momentarily, before he bites down sending a flash of exquisite pain and pleasure straight to my pussy. I gasp in need of being filled. Thoughts of Parke have filled my head from the first day I set eyes on him.

"I need to taste you, Samantha."

"Oh please, Parke, please fuck me."

"In due time, my dear. In due time," he says with a grin, kneeling down in between my legs.

"Oh God, Parke, please."

"Please what, Samantha?"

"Please fuck me."

"Oh, I will as soon as I make you come under my tongue. Be patient. You will get what we both have been waiting for."

He pulls my thong to the side and I feel his hot breath linger on my pussy for a moment. I lift my head to see what in the hell's taking him so long. He looks up at me and growls. "You are so fucking beautiful and wet for me," he says, his voice filled with lust.

I look back at him with desire and need. Recognizing my need, he puts his head between my legs and slowly licks me. He takes my clit in his mouth drawing it in with force. I arch my back in pleasure, gripping the ends of my desk and needing more. As if he can read my mind, he plunges a finger into my entrance pushing in and out as he sucks harder on my clit. I reach down and put my fingers through his hair trying to push his head down while raising my hips to get more. The combination sends me into a tailspin. I explode into a million pieces all over his face. I have not come that hard since I was center stage at a sex club with Phillip.

Parke laps softly at my slit until I stop trembling. Once I regain my bearings, I hear him fumbling in his pocket. I look up to see him rolling a condom on his long cock. The sight of his cock alone makes my pussy clench in excitement. I feel the wetness run down the crack of my ass which does not escape Parke's attention.

"Samantha, your pussy is calling for me. Do you feel it?" he asks, while capturing my wetness with his finger and sucking it into his mouth.

I moan up at him as he rubs his cock up and down my wetness.

"I felt our connection the day you walked into my office. Didn't you, Parke?"

"Yes, but I knew I needed more than one fuck with you. That's why I turned you down that day."

"And what makes you think you'll get more than this one fuck?"

He leans over pulling my earlobe into his mouth. "You already gave me more. I know you—you let me in. I know your favorite foods, your favorite drink, what makes you pissed off, and what makes you happy. I already have more, Samantha."

I look up in utter shock. He does have more. I have given him more of me than I've given any man.

"Let's just say I will give you a test run to see if you get another shot," I giggle, looking up at him.

The second the words are out of my mouth, he plunges inside of me with one hard thrust. My eyes grow wide then roll behind my lids as the pleasure is immeasurable. He raises my hips to put his cock in the right place. My knuckles are white as I grip the sides of my desk letting Parke take control of my body. His hardness is like a magic dagger filling me with pleasure.

"Samantha, how can you be this tight? You feel amazing."

A moan escapes my throat as he lifts me higher with his hands under my hips and pushes with all his might. He leans his head over and pulls my nipple into his warm lips and suckles. The sensation is too much. I can't hold on any longer. "Fuck me harder, Parke, make me come again, please," I beg

Those words push him over the edge. His pace quickens and I come undone with Parke right behind me.

He lifts his head, looks down at me, and pushes a stray hair from my face. "Why in God's name did you hold out so long? Jesus, woman, were you trying to kill me?"

I smile up at his beautiful face taking in how sexy he looks with his messy hair and flushed face. "Sorry about that. I've been pretty fucked up since I lost Phillip. I simply wasn't ready for this?"

"For what? Great sex?"

"No, for this." I point in between us. "The only way this is going to happen again is if we can both admit it."

"Admit what? That you have feelings for me? Or that I'm too damn sexy to pass up?" he says, grinning a wide smile and showing me his perfectly sexy teeth.

I turn my head looking away from him. This shit sucks. I'm not used to this feelings crap. But I'm over the one-night hook ups. Sitting home alone wishing I had someone to share my time with is getting old.

His hands cup my face bringing my attention back to him. "Just say it. I promise you won't turn to dust if you say it."

"Alright, alright, I'll say it. I have feelings for you, Parke Andrews."

His chocolate-brown eyes bore into my flesh. "And what else?"

"What else do you want me to say?"

"I want you to say you want to make a go of this. That you want to try out a relationship. One out in the open. One we don't have to hide."

"Sure, what you just said."

His eyes flash in anger. "No, ma'am, I don't think so. I don't want to waste your time, and I don't want you to waste mine. I told you I don't do hook ups. I'm too old to just play around. I really like you, Samantha, and I want to know if you're willing to make an effort for us to be a couple. Because if you can't, I'm done."

I stiffen upon hearing his ultimatum. I try to push him off so I can have some room to breathe.

"Oh no, you don't. I want you to make up your mind while I'm still deep inside of you," he says, pushing his cock farther into me. My eyes roll back in my head in both frustration and pleasure. I really do want him. I want to be with him; it's just not me to say it out loud. But hey, what the fuck. Apparently I've been doing it all wrong so I might as well try.

I look up at him with determination. "I like you, Parke, and I will do my best to have a relationship with you. But be forewarned, I really don't know how to have a normal relationship. You will have to show me the way."

"Oh, baby, I will be glad to show you the way," he mutters, kissing down my neck again.

Pulling back, I see something different in his eyes,

shame and regret. "What's wrong, Parke?" I ask, scared to hear the answer. He looks down at me in thought.

"Just spit it the fuck out, Parke," I fuss impatiently.

"Okay, understand I didn't expect to have you laid out on your desk today, or I would have prepared my speech."

"Prepared your speech? What the fuck?"

"Calm down, Samantha. I wanted you from the day I walked into this office. For your sassy cocky mouth, for your beautiful body, and for the dirty way you looked at me. I couldn't have you that day or any other day until today because ..." he says and pauses.

I don't say a word to him. I think my eyes of danger are enough.

"Damn it, I'm a cop, Samantha."

He grabs my hands quicker this time, avoiding a second slap of the night. But with both his hands on mine, he can't shield himself from my verbal slap. "You fucking bastard. You used me just to see if I was running a whorehouse, didn't you?"

He doesn't speak. He just shakes his head no.

"Fuck you, Parke, let me go."

"No. Let me finish, Samantha."

"There is nothing you can say. You're a fucking cop that has been embedded in my place of business for the sole purpose of bringing me down.

"It's not like that."

I narrow my eyes at him and try to struggle out of his grasp. "I said to fucking let me go."

"I will never be able to let you go, Samantha," he says, looking wounded. "Yes, getting info was my job. But you were never my job. I was supposed to get in and out in two weeks, but I kept putting my commander off saying I needed more time."

Through my gritted teeth, I get louder. "Get the fuck off!" He doesn't move off me, and the only thing that moves is his dick. This son of a bitch is getting hard. "I'm going to yell rape as loud as I can if you don't get off of me."

"I couldn't leave you, Samantha. I'm falling for you ..." I'm shocked by his words. "What do you mean?"

"What I mean is, I drug my two-week assignment out for four months so I could get close to you. I filed my report today with the bureau. I'm officially done here. But I don't want to be done with you. Please give me a chance."

"Why should I give you a chance? You did nothing but betray me."

"I did no such thing," he barks down at me. I didn't know you from Adam when I walked in that door. I probed your establishment because that was my job. Quickly, I learned this was not a prostitution ring nor was there anything illegal going on."

He leans down putting his forehead on mine and forcing me to look up at him. "I stayed because of you—because I was falling in love with you."

I blink not sure he just said that. "What?"

"You heard me, Samantha. Being 'just friends' forced me to see the real you, and I happen to really like the real you. Other than my occupation, I never told you a lie. Please, Samantha, give me another shot," he pleads.

I don't have any words for him and feel my heart swell from within. A single tear slides down my cheek as I shake my head yes.

He lets my arms go and wraps me into his. "I promise, I will never tell you another lie ever."

"You better not because I will fucking kill you."

He peppers kisses on my face. "I want to take you home and properly fuck you, but I have one more thing I need to share so you don't kill me.

"Oh geez," I huff out.

"No, it's not bad. I just want you to know. The bureau wants me to stay on here to keep an eye out for a suspect from St. Louis that is known to be in New Orleans, and he is known to frequent strip clubs.

"Should I be worried for my girls?"

"No, nothing like that. He's wanted on drug and racketeering charges. The FBI wants him so they can try to take down his MC club.

"As long as it does not affect my girls and you stay here to fuck me on lunch breaks, I'm good to go."

CHAPTER 16

Sunny

Mardi Gras season is in full swing. The carnival atmosphere in the city is unmistakable. It's festive and fun. The entire quarter is decorated in purple, green, and gold. The volume of people has increased dramatically in the last weekend before Mardi Gras.

Samantha and Parke finally admitted they have a thing and they're trying out being a couple. So tonight is their first time out in public as a couple. Jackson asked Sean the new bouncer to come along because Carmella thinks he's cute and we don't want her to be a third wheel.

"Okay, chick, you ready?" Carmella yells from her room.

"No, I don't know what to wear. What do you wear to a Mardi Gras parade?"

"Oh geez," I hear as the door swings open. She is in a tight pair of jeans and a casual, fitted V-neck cotton T-shirt with a light jacket and a pair of cute kid's shoes while I stand in my bra and underwear.

"Well, you could wear that and you would get a lot of beads, but I don't think Jackson would be happy," she says with a grin. "There's a lot of walking, so wear a pair of comfy shoes and bring a jacket because when the sun goes down it may be chilly."

I pull out a pair of jeans and slide them up my very narrow hips. Dancing burns a ton of calories and I have also started working out with Jackson at his gym. We have spent so much time together doing things I would have never dreamed of doing, like fishing. And he has made sure we go to the shooting range once or twice a week especially since I have my concealed weapons permit. He has been shocked at how good my aim is. I have to admit, my new gun skills amaze me as well. I feel powerful and no longer a victim.

Happy with the way the jeans fit, I thumb through my growing wardrobe for a shirt. Flipping through the hangers, I get a flash of panic. Something out of nowhere reminds me of the trackers Rex had in my clothes. I'm frozen for a moment. I hear Carmella talking to me, but I can't make out the words. I feel her hands on my shoulders shaking me.

"What the hell? Come on, we are not going to start this shit today. Turn around. Look at me."

I do as I'm told because she is pretty damn bossy, and if I don't, she will physically do it for me. I start to tell her I can't go because he may be there. But before I can get the words out, she starts to fuss.

"No fucking way. I don't want to hear it. Jackson will be there, and he would never let anything happen to you, you hear me? Not to mention Parke and Sean will be there as well. There will be so many people you may have a hard time finding me much less him finding you. Forget about him. It's been five months. If he could find you, he would have found you by now."

I take a deep breath and shake my head. "You're right." I pull her into a hug. "Thanks for always setting my ass straight."

"You betcha, that's my job. Now let me pick a shirt so we can get Samantha and meet the guys at the Casino before the parade."

She picks a snug plunging tee for me to wear with a matching light fitted jacket. "Jackson will be drooling over your cleavage all night." I smile at the warm feeling I get at the thought of Jackson inside of me and taking my nipples into his hot wet mouth.

"Oh, give me a break, and quit thinking about fucking Jackson. Have some compassion for the girl who has no one to fuck today."

I swat at her playfully. "You are a mess, girl."

"You're damn right, I'm a mess. No sex in four weeks will do that to a girl. But don't you worry, I have had my eye on Sean and I think he's into me. Or at least I think he is enough into me to knock boots tonight."

"Well, I will be at Jackson's tonight so you have the entire place to yourself. Knock away," I say, pulling her arm to the door. "Come on, I can't wait to see my man."

We find the guys playing at a roulette table in Harrah's Casino. Samantha made a reservation for us to eat a late lunch at Besh's Steakhouse. Girl has some connections because I hear the place is pretty booked twenty-four-seven. When Jackson sees me, he pulls me to him by the waist.

"Where are you going with all your shit hanging out?" he says, looking down at my shirt.

"Making sure you're still paying attention."

"Oh, I'm paying attention along with everyone else."

"Please don't tell me you're a jealous boyfriend."

He looks me up and down not really wanting to admit he's jealous.

"Of course not, just stay close to me, you hear?"

"I hear you loud and clear, captain," I say, saluting him.

"Real funny. Come on, let's go eat. I'm starving." Whispering in my ear, he continues, "And not for food, but I guess it will have to hold me over 'til later."

I reach up on my tiptoes and give him a quick kiss on his luscious lips. "Yep, it will have to hold you over because I'm going to party it up at my very first Mardi Gras parade."

He smiles down at me wrapping his arm possessively around my shoulder and pulling me toward the rest of the crew walking toward the restaurant. He looks over to me as we walk. "I got a call today."

"Oh yea, from who?"

"A friend that works in the financial aid department for Tulane University."

"What did he say?" I ask, stopping in my tracks.

"He said he received a letter from the Battered Women's shelter stating you have been approved for the Lilly Smith Funds."

"Lilly Smith Funds? What is that?"

"It's a college fund that the battered women's shelter sponsors, and they choose one candidate each year to put through college. They chose you."

"Me, why me?"

"Because you're worth it, Sunny. Why not you?" he asks, framing my face with his hands.

I look down at the ground.

"Damn it, Sunny, when are you going to realize that? You are worth it! You are a smart woman that deserves to fulfill her dreams of becoming a nurse, and some coward asshole that hits women should not stop you from doing that."

He pulls me into his hard chest. "Do you believe me, Sunny? Don't you believe you're worth it?"

I look up with tears in my eyes. No one has ever called me smart much less said I was worth it. And he is right, I am worth it. Tears of joy slide down my cheeks. "I am worth it, Jackson. Thank you for helping me see that and most of all with all the paper work to get enrolled in school. I could not have done it without you," I say, putting my lip on his. I don't care who's watching me kiss him madly like a teenager. I'm absolutely in love with this man. Now is not the time to tell him, but I will tell him soon.

Walking to our table, Carmella shouts, "Can y'all keep your hands off of each other long enough to eat?"

"Hell no," I respond with a happy grin, sitting in the chair Jackson has pulled out for me. The waiter has already filled our glasses with wine so I stand and lift my glass to everyone in a toast. "I want to take a minute to be all sappy."

"Aw shit, I hate sappy, you know that," Samantha complains with Carmella agreeing.

I blow her a kiss. "I know you hate it, but you will have to grin and bear it. First of all, I want to thank you, Samantha, for giving me a job and putting me in Jackson's path." I turn and look to him as he looks back with genuine love.

"You're going to make me gag," Samantha says jokingly. She shuts up quickly when Parke's hand mysteriously disappears under the table and she yelps.

"I got this, Sunny. Continue your speech, baby girl," Parke says proudly. Samantha does not say another word. She just grins.

"Thanks, Parke. Because I want to say thanks to Carmella for always helping me keep my shit together when I lose it. And most of all, I want to thank this fine hunk of a man sitting here."

He actually looks embarrassed. He pulls on my hand in an attempt to make me sit down. "No, Jackson, I'm not done. I have always wanted to go to college and to become a nurse, but I never had the know-how to get it done. And you see, this man not only encouraged me to follow my dreams, but he helped me complete enrollment papers and grant papers, and today he got the call."

They all look on in excitement when I shout, "I got accepted to Tulane University on a full paid grant for four years."

The table erupts in cheers. Carmella gets out of her chair almost knocking me over in a great big hug. "I knew you could do it." She leaves my side and wraps Jackson into a hug that clearly makes him cutely uncomfortable. "You are exactly what she needed. But you better do her right or I will kick your ass. You hear me?"

"Loud and clear," he says, putting some distance between them.

It was a great start to a great night. Our late lunch is filled with laughs and non-stop drinks. Carmella and Sean seem to be hitting it off nicely, and Samantha and Parke are chummy as well. I look around at everyone, and being in a thankful mood, I send a special thank you up to God and Joe once again for taking me out of the claws of Rex and placing me in the path of my newfound family. At this moment, I officially bury Rex in my memory. He is dead to me, and I will never speak another word of him.

After stopping at the Daiquiris shop to get some frozen drinks for the parade, we're off. Samantha had scored six tickets for the parade stands in front of the Intercontinental Hotel. People are everywhere, and the crowd is so thick, the closer we get to the route, the thicker the crowd gets. And the thicker the crowd gets, the more my hair stands on edge. I'm not sure what the problem is, so why do I feel this way? I just have a feeling in my gut that we are being followed. I know it's crazy but I feel it. I start to nervously look around to see if I see anyone with an MC cut.

Looking around, I only see people partying and having fun. Some are dressed in costume, most in Mardi Gras colors, but all have beads draped around their necks having a good time.

Shake it off. You are just being crazy," I think and suck down more of my frozen drink. We reach the stands where we'll be viewing the parade. I know it is about to start when I see flashing lights coming and hear music. Once it starts, it's the most amazing thing I have ever seen and heard. The first band passes and it's not what I expected. I expected what you see on TV for the Macy's Thanksgiving Day parade. Nope, it was like nothing I've ever seen. The first band is a high school band all dancing in unison as they play an upbeat song that has everyone bouncing in the stands. The cheerleaders and dancers are getting down with more soul than you would think was possible at their young age. The crowd erupts in cheers as they pass. The floats start to pass starting with the King and Queen. They are dressed in sparkly beaded costumes with large feathered plumes that come from their shoulders and reach two to three feet above their heads. They wave diamond-encrusted wands to the crowd.

Once the court has passed, the real floats start to roll. I have only heard of Mardi Gras, but to see it in person is breathtaking. The costumes are elaborate, the bands are energetic, and the way the crowd erupts when the floats pass is invigorating. Their hands go up in the air, and they all scream, "Throw me something, mister." The entire experience is electric and so much fun. To see the excitement on the faces of the children when they catch something worth keeping is priceless.

Midway through the parade, the feeling of being watched has subsided. But to be honest with myself, I'm not sure if it's because of the booze or there is just too much going on to care. This is the Big Easy, and people tend to just let the good times roll, so I go with the flow ignoring the whispering in my gut telling me to be alert and aware.

The parade is over and the crowd starts to disburse in all directions. But Carmella and Samantha are far from done for the night.

"Let's go to Cat's," Carmella yells, tugging on Sean's arm. The poor kid looks like a lost puppy willing to follow her to the ends of the earth.

Samantha is giving Parke puppy eyes, as he doesn't look too interested in the idea. She whispers something in his ear and his face lights up.

"Okay, just a few songs and then were gone," he says, while grabbing Samantha by the waist and pulling her into a deep kiss for everyone to see.

"Get a room, y'all," Carmella hollers. "Let's get going." She turns to Jackson. "Are you two in or what?"

Jackson answers for me, "Just a few songs then were done."

I shake my head in confirmation. We're having a great time and I hate to leave, but I have to admit, I would much rather be rolling around in bed with Jackson right now.

We start pushing through the crowd when I notice Jackson seems a bit antsy. He's looking around a lot and his grip on my hand has tightened. We're moving pretty fast through the people, and it's so loud he doesn't hear me talking. By the time we make it to Cat's on Bourbon Street, I'm beat from being pulled though the crowd.

"Is everything okay, Jackson," I ask, out of breath.

"Yeah, why?"

I shrug my shoulders not wanting to make a big thing about it, but the feeling of being watched has definitely resurfaced on our way to Cat's.

"Just asking. You seemed to be a bit antsy while moving through the crowds."

He pulls me in and kisses the top of my head not wanting to look at me when he replies, "Sometimes crowds make me uneasy, you know, ever since Iraq. Shit always went down in the middle of heavily crowded marketplaces, and it just makes me aware. Sorry, I didn't mean to make you nervous."

I look up at him forcing him to look down at me. "I would never be nervous when I'm with you. And I can't imagine the terror of being in such a horrible place."

"Come on, let's get in and get out as soon as possible. I want you naked in my bed," he says, nipping at the sensitive skin behind my ear.

I giggle and pull him inside the club. The group is

already at the bar ordering more drinks. Carmella walks my way with a cosmopolitan. She knows my weakness. I raise my finger up at her. "Just one and then were gone."

"Oh come on, let's have a good time. Jackson can have you in his bed every night after this."

She's right, and I haven't told her yet, but Jackson asked me to move in with him, and I don't think I can go much longer without sharing his bed daily. I turn to Jackson with my drink in hand. "Look, as much as I really want to be in bed with you, let's hang with everyone for a little bit more than one drink. Please?"

I wrap my free hand around his waist pulling him against my body. "On our next weekend off, I want to take you up on that offer to move into your place if that's still on the table, and—"

Before I get any more words out, his mouth crashes down on mine. His lips are possessive and needy. As he sucks my bottom lip into his mouth, his eyes stare back at mine. Slowly he releases me. "It's still on the table. You had about one more week to do it, or I was going to move you there and not let you go anyway."

His eyes are soft and happy now. My Jackson, Mr. Serious, looks happy and relieved.

"We work this weekend, and I have some shit to take care of next week, but the following weekend, it's a done deal, babe."

I feel almost giddy. He warms me from inside out, and I'm so lucky to have found him. I kiss him quickly and shout to the group, "Let's dance!" Everyone follows, bumping and grinding with our guys. Carmella looks to be having a good time with Sean, and Samantha and Parke are crazy in lust with each other. I'm not quite sure I would call it love yet, but I think if she lets her heart open, they will be well on their way.

After a few drinks, a bathroom break is required. Tugging Carmella from Sean's lips was a feat, but she eventually comes. As we walk, I get an overwhelming feeling I'm being watched and followed AGAIN. I stop in my tracks, terrified to turn around. Carmella runs into the back of me. "What the fuck?"

I'm frozen. I can't turn. I just know he must be there. I feel the hate. Carmella is now in front of me. "What the hell are you doing? I thought you had to go to the bathroom. You pulled me away from a luscious pair of lips."

I stare up at her in total fear. "Please look behind us and tell me you don't see anyone with a leather motorcycle cut watching us. Carmella, I just have a bad feeling. Tell me you don't see anyone."

I see her eyes scanning the room with true concern.

"Honey, I don't see anyone that remotely looks like a biker. I do see some bitch eyeing us up, but I noticed her ass earlier. She's just hating because our men are hot and her stupid ass is alone."

"Are you sure?"

She turns me by the shoulders. "Yes, I'm sure. No one but that dagger-eyed bitch," she says, pointing to a blonde woman looking at us with sheer hate. I've never seen her before so I assume she's drunk and has us mistaken with someone else.

"Oh God, thanks, Carmella. What the hell is her problem?"

"I don't know, but if she is still there when we come out, she'll wish she wasn't." Carmella flips her the bird forcing the woman to turn around.

"You see, she don't want a piece of this," she says, motioning to herself. "I will tear that bitch up."

I laugh a deep belly laugh as Carmella is a little small thing, but I would not want to tangle with her. She is full of tattoos and looks a bit intimidating in a beautiful tough girl way.

"Let's go before I piss on myself."

"Oh, Carmella, we have to work on your lady-like manners."

"Alright, Mom, let's get in line."

When we return from the restroom, the blonde is nowhere in sight. My feeling of being watched is gone so I chalk it up to the crazy blonde. We return to Jackson and Sean, but Samantha and Parke are nowhere to be found.

"Okay, who let the lust birds get away?"

Raising his hands, Jacksons says, "I didn't know we were to hold them prisoners."

"Real funny, Mr. Wise Guy," Carmella retorts.

"You ready, babe?" Jackson asks, while nodding his head at me and letting me know this is really not a question.

I turn to Carmella. "Okay, party girl, I've had enough dancing for the night. I'm going home for the real fun."

"Home, since when is his place home? Are you trying to tell me something?"

I smile at her trying to soften the blow. "You knew it was only a matter of time." Pulling her into a hug, I whisper in her ear, "Thanks for all you've done for me, but I'm in love with him."

She pulls away with a smile on her face looking at mine. "No shit, Sherlock, I'm just gonna miss you."

"Not this weekend but next, so we have plenty of girl time, okay?"

"Okay, meanwhile, I will enjoy Sean tonight at the apartment without having to keep my screams down," she says with a wink.

"Have fun and be safe," I say with raised eyebrows.

"Don't worry, I always have raincoats in my purse."

We say our goodbyes and head back to Jackson's place on the water. The drinks really hit me hard on the ride over there. I had more than I thought and don't feel so well.

When we arrive, Jackson looks over at me. "Are you going to be okay? You don't look so good?"

"I'm not sure? I think I just have to lie down for a

moment."

He looks at me with a sad smile.

"As soon as the world stops spinning, I will feel better and we'll have wild sex, I promise."

He comes over to my side of the Jeep and opens the door. Lifting me out of the car, he brings me in and puts me down on his bed gently. "Come on, girl, the wild sex can wait to the morning."

He takes off my shoes and my clothes slowly trying to avoid moving me too much. When he starts to slip off my panties, I look up at him in surprise. "I thought you said it was gonna wait?"

He chuckles, "I want you ready in the morning. Now let me get the bra, and I'll be back with some water and Advil.

I'm almost out when he returns. I sit slowly, take what he's offering, and lie back down. I feel him get in on the other side gently pulling me to him. My naked back is against his naked front and it feels like heaven. His arms wrap around me as I drift off feeling so loved.

When I wake, we are in the same position. But I hear his breathing and know he's awake. Just his breathing turns me on. He's waiting for me to wake up. I feel his glorious morning wood pressing into my naked ass. I push my rear back on him with a wiggle letting him know I'm awake. He grunts pulling me toward him tightly.

"You finally awake, babe? How you feel?"

I don't turn to him because I really need to get out of bed and brush my teeth. I got in bed last night without brushing and that is just gross.

"I feel better than expected."

"I will let you know how you feel," he says, swiping his finger through my welcoming wetness making me moan aloud. The things this man does to me. Just hearing him breathe in my ear and feeling his hardness causes me to pool in wetness. Before I can react, his finger plunges inside of me.

"Oh, Jackson, that feels amazing, but I really have to brush my teeth."

"Fuck no, not letting you go, babe. Newsflash, I don't give a shit about your teeth. I'm gonna take you from back here. Brush when we're done."

I should be pissed that he is always ordering me around in the bedroom, but it's just too damn hot. My brain shuts off all logical thought when he slides another finger into me. He now has two fingers in and his pinky brushes my clit and his thumb grazes my rear. The anticipation of what he is going to do with that thumb has me on edge. His pace quickens and my orgasm hits me with its usual stars and full-body tingling. The tingling radiates though my limbs. I put my hand over his trying to stop the movement. I need a moment to catch my breath.

He rolls over to the nightstand and reaches for a condom when I grab his hand. "You don't need it."

"What? Are you sure?"

"Yes, I've been on the pill right over thirty days so you're good," I say, smiling at him over my shoulder.

His eyes turn dark and full of want. I turn back over inviting him back into the same position. Instantly, I feel his heated skin on mine pulling me in close and tight. His hardness rubs in between my wetness, but he doesn't enter me. He just slides it up and down driving me insane.

"Jackson, please?"

"Please what, Sunny?"

I wait in silence praying he gives me what I need without making me beg for it.

"Do you know how long I have waited to slide my bare cock into that sweet pussy of yours?"

Again, I say nothing and let him talk. His voice is so husky and smooth.

"From the moment I saw you standing on the street, I knew I needed you." His arms are wrapped around my body pulling me in so tight. It's like he feels frightened to let me go. "And when you started thinking about bolting, I saw it in your eyes. I knew you were going to walk out of my life, and I couldn't let that happen. So tell me you want me inside of you, Sunny. I want to hear you say it. But know the second I slide my bare dick inside of you, you're mine. I won't ever let you go. Do you understand that?"

I turn my head back to see his face. How could he not already know?

"I have been yours since that day." I wrap my hand around myself and over his arms. "I want to feel you and only you inside of me, Jackson. Please, please give me all of you because you have all of me."

He thrusts inside of me with one slow motion. I moan in pleasure with Jackson groaning behind me. His movements are slow and steady; he fills me deeper with every push. My skin is on fire with the sensation of being owned by him, and it pushes me to new heights. His fingers find my nipple and he slowly twists it with the methodically slow motion he's using to move in and out of me. Even with my back to him, I feel so close to him. The slowness is tender until his other hand grasps onto my clit and his pace quickens. His thrusts are coming harder and my need to come is growing more intense. My breathing always gives me away.

"Wait for me, Sunny. Feel me, feel every inch of what's yours and only yours."

"Please, Jackson, harder."

He lets up on my nipple and clit to hold onto my hips and gives it to me harder. I'm about to come undone when he lets go of my hips to circle my clit with the exact amount of pressure needed. My screams of his name are followed by his grunting of mine.

What a beautiful morning.

CHAPTER 17

Sunny

"Girl, you must be killing it with tips this week," Carmella says, excitedly putting on my makeup for my shift tonight. It's the Monday before Mardi Gras and everyone is feeling festive. "The weather has been great, and they said this may be the busiest Mardi Gras in years." She loves to chat and make small talk, but I'm not interested. All I can think about is Jackson.

I look up at her with a glow. Work has been great. The club has been packed with tons of out-of-towners, and the money has been plentiful. But most of all, I just can't wipe the smile off my face thinking of where my relationship is with Jackson. It's perfect. Tomorrow is Mardi Gras and they said things will calm down. I work this coming weekend, and then next weekend, I will officially move in with him.

"There you go again daydreaming on me," she says, slapping my arm.

"Ouch, what the hell, girl."

"You make me sick with that 'I'm in love' grin all the time," she replies, laughing.

"Don't hate on me. I didn't tell you to drop Sean, or Kevin, for that matter. Why did you do that anyway?"

"Because he is too damn nice. I need it a little tougher in the bedroom. You know what I mean?"

Flashes of Jackson demanding a certain position from me has my panties wet instantly. I blush When I answer her. "Yes, I know what you mean."

"Exactly, Mr. Nice guy is too sweet in the sack."

"I'm sorry, Carmella, you'll find him. I promise. Your Mr. Right will come along."

"I hope to hell he does before I'm too old. Now get your ass out there. You have five minutes."

I blow her a kiss not wanting to mess up my lipstick and rush out the door to the club. Tonight I'm dancing on the boxes, which is always fun. It's easy money dancing up there and having a good time while people throw you money.

Tonight we have on Mardi Gras themed outfits that are a bit more risqué than Samantha usually has us in, but hey, isn't Mardi Gras a bit more risqué than a regular day? The top is a beaded purple halter with gold accents, and the bottom is a beaded green thong accented in gold. We have never worn a thong in the club before, but its suggestiveness is muted a bit by the thick, shiny nude stockings underneath.

Walking out into the club, I feel as if I'm walking on air. My life has come full circle and I'm just so happy. The room is crowded as I walk to my box. When I feel a heavy hand gripping my shoulder, all of the blood rushes from my face and I freeze, not fighting it. I am pulled behind a large column near my box and out of sight from security. When I look up, I'm shocked to see the face staring back at me. It takes me a moment to even process it. It's the blonde from Cat's and she looks deranged. Her hair is a mess, her eyes are wild, and she looks like she has not slept in weeks.

"Let me go. What do you want, who are you?" I shout over the music with a shaky voice.

"Oh, has your precious Jackson not told you about me?"

I look at her confused. Jackson has not said anything about a crazy woman. His sister did mention the last relationship did not work out well but that is it. My lack of knowledge sets her off.

"You fucking whore. Of course, he never told you about me. You're just a good fuck to him. Why would he bother telling you about us? What we have is special and real, unlike you," she snarls with anger.

Now she has pissed me off. "What do you mean us?"

"Oh dear, dear. Enjoy him while it lasts because after Monday, he'll be all mine," she chuckles, letting go of her guard and my arm.

The rage fills me thinking Jackson would leave me for her. The second my arm is free, it comes across her face hard and loud. Her head snaps back in surprise. However, she doesn't move, and she still has me boxed in behind the column.

"You stupid bitch. You see, Jackson and I were together for almost a year, and one day, he drank a bit too much." She looks down lost in thought. "He didn't mean to do it, but he did."

"Did what?"

"Well, I pushed him too far and made him angry. It really was all my fault. I made him do it."

"Pushed him to do what?" I don't like what she's implying. Jackson could never.

As if she could read my mind, she says, "Yes, he hit me."

I gasp and cover my mouth with my hand in shock. She has to be lying. I stand in shock as she reaches into her bag and pulls out her phone.

"You see what he did to me!" she screams in anger as she flips through pictures on her phone. Her face is battered and bruised to the point it is almost unrecognizable. But she has a tattoo on her collarbone with Jackson's name that matches the one I see when I look back down at her. He could not have done this to her. Jackson would never put a hand on me like Rex, could he?

As my doubt rises, she shoves the final dagger into me. She flips to another picture. It's a news article showing Jackson in handcuffs with the title, "Ranger beats girlfriend unconscious." My heart instantly shatters into a million pieces as I stand there staring at the image. It's Jackson with his head hung low and walking in handcuffs. Her wicked voice pulls my attention away from the image and into her cruel wild eyes.

"The trial is next Monday, and if he promises to take me back, I won't press charges." She smirks an evil grin and licks her painted lips as she steps away from me.

I walk past her with a push. I have nothing left to say to her. When I shrug past her, she says, "Tell Jackson Norma says she misses him."

I think I may throw up. What in the hell just happened to me? I refuse to fall apart and cry. That's the old me and I refuse to do it. I will not allow another man to make me crumble. I march up to the bar and see Sean working. I motion him over to me. "Two shots of vodka."

"Are you okay, Sunny?"

"Yeah, I just need two shots. Is that a problem?" I say in an ugly tone.

He holds his hands up in surrender. "No, no, I'm sorry. You just looked upset, that's all." He turns and pours me two shots. I throw them back one after another and walk off without another word. I'll pay him later.

I do my best to push it out of my head while I'm on the box. The place is packed and I can't leave Samantha hanging tonight. I just have to suck it up. It feels like it takes forever for my shift to be over. When it is, I rush to get changed trying to avoid Carmella and Jackson. If I see either of them, I will fall apart. I manage to get out without either of them seeing me. Jackson is busy with the rowdy crowd and Carmella is busy reapplying Dixie's makeup before her double shift. I asked her to step in for me telling her I didn't feel well.

I run out the back door and immediately feel the regret for leaving without confronting Jackson. But what is there to talk about? I ran from a man that was going to beat me to death if I stayed. I can't be with a man that I know may snap. I grasp my jacket and wrap myself tight trying to stay warm on the walk home.

The streets are busy, but damn it, I know better than

to walk home alone. I hear voices and see shadows behind me. *Your mind is playing tricks on you,* I think and pick up the pace. I roll my eyes as I start to hear the Voodoo Queen's voice in my head. *"The tiger is the only thing that can save you from the dragon."* I cringe at the memory of her saying that. But the words keep playing in my head as I hear footsteps getting closer. I'm half a block away from Carmella's apartment when the person is so close to me I can hear their breath behind me. When I start to sprint, a large strong hand grabs me. I try to scream but the other hand covers my mouth.

The arms turn me and bring me into an embrace. "Shhh, it's just me," Jackson says. "It's okay, Sunny. You have to listen to me. Please don't scream, but I can't watch you run away from me. I saw that crazy bitch Norma at the club, and she told me what she said to you. I need you to know it's a lie."

I look at him with an enormous amount of fear. How can I not considering my past and what she showed me? I don't want to talk to him right now. I can't.

"Let me go now," I say loudly.

"No, you need to hear me out."

I raise my voice even louder this time, "Let me go now!" That was loud enough to draw the attention of a uniformed police officer that has just rounded the corner. "Is there a problem here, Miss?"

Jackson loosens his grip on me as the officer approaches.

"I think I heard the lady ask you to let her go," he says sternly with his hand on his hip near his gun.

"Sir, this is my girlfriend, and we were just having a bit of a discussion."

I look at the officer. "I am his ex-girlfriend, and I'm not interested in having a discussion with him. Could you please make sure he stands here while I get into my apartment?"

"Ma'am, do you want to make a report? Did he hurt you?"

My face flames red. He has not only hurt me, but he has broken me into tiny pieces. I love him, but I have to walk away from him.

"No, sir, he has not touched me. I just want to go home without him."

"I understand. Sir, stand back. You and I are going to have a little chat while she walks home."

I turn and run, not looking back. Once inside the apartment, I lock myself in my room and slide down the door in a ball and cry. I must sit there for over an hour until I hear Carmella unlock the front door. I jump into bed and cover my face pretending to be asleep.

I know she will check on me and she does. The light peeks in as she opens the door, "Poor baby must be getting the flu," I hear her say softly. She shuts the door, and I sigh in relief that I don't have to talk about it right now. I need to get it together and put up a wall tomorrow. I don't want to crumble and put myself in the same position as in the past. I spend the night tossing and turning and finally fall to exhaustion around 6:00 a.m.

When I wake, Carmella sits cross-legged on the sofa in her pajamas. She looks up at me with a sympathetic smile. "How you feeling this morning? Any better?"

I walk over to her and sit beside her. "I don't feel any better. But I'm not sick, I don't have the flu."

"Then what's wrong, honey?" She puts her hand on my leg.

I tell her about my encounter with Norma at the club last night. She pulls me into a big hug and doesn't let go for a long moment waiting for me to break down in my usual way. She pulls back surprised that I'm not hysterical.

With a crossed look on her face, she asks, "Are you sure you are okay? I don't see one tear, and honey, that kinda scares me."

"I know but I cried everything I had last night, and I just don't have any more left to cry. I can't do it again so I have to be strong. I decided I'm going to give my notice and waitress somewhere until school starts. I already have the grant for school, so I really just need money to be able to help you with rent here." I look up at her with pleading eyes. "That is, if you are okay with me staying with you a little longer."

Swatting her hand at me, she says, "Of course, that is not even a question. You are always welcome here. But honey, don't you think you should at least hear his side?"

Before I can protest, she gives me the death glare—the hear me out or I may slap you look.

"I'm just saying I saw that girl at Cat's. She had crazy written all over her. It may not be what it seems, that's all."

"I don't know?"

The days run together like molasses, slow and thick. The day after the Norma incident, Jackson came to the apartment, but I told Carmella not to let him in, I didn't want to see him or hear him out. I had Carmella tell Samantha I was not coming back and why. I knew she would understand, but I do feel bad just walking out like that. I just can't face him yet; I can't walk into the club and see him without folding. I need more time to build up my shield. And when my shield is hardened, I'll go back to the club, but only to get the few things I left there. I left my grandmother's heart locket in my locker when I ran out without putting it back on. I feel naked without it, but I never danced with it on since I was afraid I would lose it. Maybe tomorrow I can go in. *Who are you kidding? It will take years to get over Jackson and the deception of who he really is.*

Mardi Gras day has come and gone with me shriveled up in a ball on the sofa. Carmella tried to get me to go to the final parade of the Mardi Gras season with her, but I was not in the mood. I turned my cell phone off the night I left Jackson standing on the street with the police officer and have not had the heart to turn it back on. I miss Jackson so much, but I can't willingly go back to a man that has ever laid a hand on a woman. That is what I'm running from. I can't bring myself to run to it, no matter how much my heart hurts to have him in my arms and in my bed.

The sun starts to go down and I figure I need to get out of bed and try to eat something for the first time today. The loss of Jackson still makes my stomach roll, but I manage to nibble on some toast and peanut butter. Carmella is out with Dixie looking for a new man. I think I have been lying in this bed forever. In reality, I think it has been four full days and five nights straight. Carmella may physically pull me out tomorrow morning; she's lost her patience with my moping. But hell, she has not had her heart ripped out and stomped on, so I will sit here and have my own personal pity party as long as I like.

I shove a piece of toast in my mouth when I hear a loud thud on the door. I get up quickly to see who's banging on the door. But as soon as I do, the rooms starts to spin and I see spots. *Damn it, I'm going down.* I do my best to get to the ground before it happens.

"Sunny, open the door. I know you are in there. I hear you breathing, Sunny." I hear him beg as my eyes open, and I look up at the fourteen-foot ceiling.

"Please, Sunny, listen to me. It's not what you think, I promise. Hear me out. Open the door, Sunshine, please," he pleads.

I had managed to get down pretty close to the ground before I went out, so I don't think I hurt anything. I sit up slowly and kneel before I try to get up. Once I'm up, I walk quietly to the door and place my hands flat on the door trying to feel him. Knowing he's out there pains my heart. He is begging me to open the door, but I just can't do it. I owe Joe and myself too much to do it. I turn and walk away with tears streaming down my face. I can't listen to his voice. It's too much, and I will crumble. I make my way to the bathroom flipping on the vent and the shower trying to drown out the noise.

As I undress, I can still hear him out there, but at least, I can't hear the words, or the lies. I get undressed and catch my pathetic reflection in the mirror. I have not eaten a real meal or seen the sun in four days. My sleep has been nonexistent, and it clearly shows with dark circles under my eyes. My hair is greasy, and I've lost a few pounds. I look like I did when I was with Rex, broken. The image pisses me off. How did I let another man do this to me? *How?* I stare at my reflection for a moment longer deciding the pity party is officially over.

I get into the shower and take a very long time washing myself and trying to feel new again. I wash myself and my hair two or three times each, hoping Jackson will be gone when I get out. Shutting the water off, I step out and listen. It's silent, and I try to tell myself I'm happy he's gone. I take my time blow-drying my hair, putting lotion on my freshly shaven legs, and putting on some tinted moisturizer to make me feel better about the circles under my eyes.

I step out of the bathroom heading straight to the front door to check the peephole. He is gone and a mixture of emotions flood my mind and heart. I shove them all away determined to get it together. Picking up the remote, I flip on the TV to have some noise while I go back to the kitchen. I need more to eat if I don't want to keep passing out every time I stand. One of the best things about living with Carmella is her mom's cooking. She brings us containers of food every Sunday. I had overheard her mom say she made me some special corn and crab soup since I wasn't feeling well.

I open the fridge in search of her Ms. Marie's delicious

soup. After two bowls of the creamy delight, I truly feel better already, inside and out. I figured while I was at it, I would try her homemade chocolate éclairs since I was down a few pounds anyway. I take one bite and moan as the smooth cream invades my senses.

"Well, that sounds better than sex," Carmella teases from the open door.

"It's gonna have to be," I say, looking back down to my éclair.

Striding over to the table, she gets a good glance at my cleaned-up self. "Hot damn, woman, you finally got your dirty ass in the shower."

I look up at her with daggers and then smirk at her playfully. "When the pounding on the door by Jackson started, I had to get away so the shower was the only place I could go to block it out."

I pop the last piece of heaven in my mouth and ask with a mouthful, "Have wine with me?"

"Considering I'm home from a night out at 9:00 p.m. with you and not some hot piece of ass, I really should drink myself into a stupor."

We laugh and drink until the three bottles of wine are empty. It felt good to laugh, be silly, and forget about Jackson, even if it were only for a few hours. And for the first time in days, I sleep soundly.

The next morning, I get up and pour myself some coffee.

"Ya finally up?" Carmella asks from the couch. "You look good. You look like you have finally rested."

"I am rested and I really do feel better. I think I feel well enough to run into the club and empty my locker. Do you know if Jackson is working today?"

"I don't know if he's working, but I have seen him, and he doesn't look good, Sunny. You think you looked like shit, he looked just as bad if not worse."

"Really," I say with both sadness and pleasure that I'm

not the only one suffering.

"Yes, really, and he has asked me about you every time I see him. I think you should hear him out."

I look up at her with shock. Whose side is she on? As the words leave her mouth, there is a knock at the door. We both look at each other knowing who's probably on the other side of the door. Carmella gets up and goes to the door. Before she reaches it, she looks back at me. "I won't leave you so please just hear him out. I will be on the other side of the paper-thin wall, and girl, you know I have your back." Smiling at me, she looks through the peephole. Looking back at me, she shrugs as if she does not know who it is.

"Who is it?" Carmella shouts at the door.

"It's Melinda," the person from outside yells.

Carmella whispers to me, "Do you know a Melinda?"

I get up and walk past her to look through the hole.

"It's Jackson's sister," I say in shock.

"Come on, Sunny, hear me out," she shouts through the door. "You asked me how you can repay me for removing your tattoo, and now I'm here to collect. Just hear me out. That's all I ask of you."

I push Carmella to the side and open the door. Melinda steps in looking around at our small apartment.

"Hey," I say shyly. I didn't expect her, and I'm not sure what she's doing here. "Sorry, I wasn't expecting you."

"Yeah, I figured that, but I really need to talk to you," she says, looking up to Carmella.

Carmella being Carmella does not back down. She steps toward Melinda with her hand out. "Hi. I'm Carmella, Sunny's best friend and roommate."

"Hi. I'm Jackson's sister Melinda, nice to meet you. But if you don't mind, I would really like to talk to Sunny in private."

"Not a problem. I was about to go take a shower and get dressed anyway. Call me if you need me, honey."

"I will," I say to her as she walks away to the bathroom and gives me a smile.

"Look, Sunny, I don't want to waste your time, and you have met me enough times to know I'm not going to bullshit you."

I look down at my hands, wringing them together and feeling exposed. How much does she really know about Jackson and me?

"Sunny, please look at me. I care about you, and I love my brother. This is crazy. That fucking bitch Norma has been a thorn in his side since the day he met her."

"So he just beat the shit out of her because she deserved it," I say with wide eyes and discontent dripping from my words.

She stiffens in her chair looking at me square on. "I understand how upset you are—"

"Do you really, Melinda? Has anyone ever beat the crap out of you? Has a man ever laid hands on you? Because if not, you don't understand how upset I am."

She reaches over and places her hand on mine. "Please listen to the truth. I promise you will understand. I will give it to you short and sweet. "

I shake my head in confirmation, and she begins her story.

"Jackson came home from his tour and he was a mess. The shit they see over there will fuck you up. And he did everything and anything in the ways of a woman to try and forget the pain. When Norma got her hooks into him, she knew she had a good thing, and she didn't want to let him go. Jackson was not the man you know today when he let her into his life. He was a shell of a man during that time in his life. But being the man he is, he rebounded and realized she was a nut job. He broke it off with her, and she just kept coming back."

The more she speaks, the angrier I get. Is she really about to tell me this chick deserved it? If she does, I may not be able to handle it.

"Don't look at me like that, Sunny. You said you would hear me out."

"Then please get to the short of it."

"So that's when he bought the place near the lake so he could get away from her. Be away from the city and do the things he liked. You ever notice you don't have cell service out there?"

"What?" I'm confused as to why she would ask. Of course, I noticed. As soon as you get within five miles of the area, the phone goes out. It annoyed me because my own cell phone was new to me, but Jackson would always say how peaceful it was not be hooked up to technology.

"Cell service," she repeats, trying to make me understand.

"Yes, I know what you are talking about, but what does that have to do with anything?"

"It was just another way to cut his ties with her. He changed his number, but she always seemed to find it. So no cell service, and he even moved jobs so there was no way for her to find him. Anyway, she finally found out where he worked and waited for him outside. She started a fight on purpose in front of the security cameras. She pushed his buttons about his tour, and then she physically attacked him. He did not hit her, Sunny. He never hit her. He was able to restrain her, which does not look really nice on camera, but he never hit her. She went home that night and paid someone to beat the shit out of her, and she blamed it on my brother."

I give her a questioning look. "You have to admit, Melinda, that sounds a bit convoluted, don't you think?"

"Absofuckinglutely … I about tore Jackson a new asshole when it went down. But he has never lied to me in our entire lives. I would know it."

"But I'm not his twin, and I have not known him my entire life. How can you expect me to believe this?"

"I would never ask you to believe it if it weren't true. I received a call and this information from the FBI last night. Here take a look."

She shoves her phone in my hand and presses play. Immediately, I recognize that blonde bitch Norma. Her face is plastered with makeup, and her silicone-inflated lips are painted the same red as the other night. She's facing the camera and speaking to a man. What she says is earth shattering. In her evil voice, she says, "I paid you $1,000 to beat the shit out of me to make it look like my boyfriend Jackson did it, and now you want to charge me $10,000 to keep it a secret?"

I cover my mouth in horror gasping at the thought that someone would do such a thing. I saw the pictures of her. She was beaten so badly she was almost unrecognizable.

"Oh, wait, there is more. You need to see the next one. Flip to the next video, Sunny."

I do as she instructs. The next one is still her face, but the unseen man is speaking, and what he says is even more shocking if that's possible. "You see, Norma, I actually filmed me beating you." She gasps knowing her house of cards could fall at any moment. Then he proceeds to speak. "You see, I owe a lot of money to a bookie, so either you get it today, or I will sell it to Jackson for his court date. Either way, I will make ten grand today."

The reaction on her face is pure evil. "I will get you your damn money, but I need more time."

"How much you have in that pretty little purse of yours to hold me over?"

"What?"

"You fucking heard me. I need a down payment."

She fumbles through her purse coming out with a couple hundred dollars. As soon as the money hits his hands, you see the bodies in the background moving quickly to the car. The door flies open and the new voices scream, "FBI, you're under arrest."

They pull Norma out of the car by the arm and handcuff her right there as she screams at the unknown apparently undercover man trying to save his ass from beating her in the first place for money.

My heart is beating out of my chest. I feel the hot tears pouring down my face in relief. Will he forgive me for not hearing him out? I'm now scared I may have lost him.

"Sleazy fucking bitch. I could not stand that girl from the very first day I met her," Melinda says, taking the phone from my hand.

"Go to him, Sunny! He understands how this looks, and to tell you the truth, without this video, he was going to jail. He was not going to cave to her demand of being with her. He told me if he didn't have you, he would rather be in jail.

I look up with a glimmer of hope. "He still wants me?"

"Does he still want you? The man can't function without you. He's a wreck. Come on, get dressed and I'll bring you to the club."

I stand up giving her a tight hug. "Thanks for showing me."

"I'm just glad this slimy bastard that beat the shit out of her needed an out and sang like a canary to get her locked up. She was arrested last night. I have my DVR set for the noon news because I can't wait to see them parade her ass in front of the cameras."

I feel my insides flutter knowing I can have Jackson back in my life. I run off to my room, throw on a dress, slap on some quick makeup, throw my hair in a messy bun, and grab my purse to head out the door with Melinda.

CHAPTER 18

Sunny

Melinda drops me off at the front of the club knowing Jackson is in his office. The club isn't open yet, but Samantha sees me at the door and unlocks it.

"Girl, your ass better be here to cheer up that poor man of yours. He looks like shit, you know?"

I smile at her feeling a little embarrassed I didn't come in and tell her I was quitting.

"Look, I wanted to tell you I'm sorry I had to quit the way I did."

"Don't worry about shit like that, girl. I like you and really didn't want you stripping anyway. You have dreams, and you need to follow them. But most importantly, follow that hunk of man that is so head over heels for you he can't even do his job."

"That's what I'm here for. Where is he?"

"The same place he has been for the last four days, sulking in his office."

I rush to the back of the building to Jackson's office and knock on the door. When he doesn't respond, I try the knob. It's unlocked so I slowly push the door open. My heart sinks and dread fills me that I have done this to him. It's just past noon, and he has a bottle of Crown in one hand and the other laying lifelessly on his desk. Not much has been removed from the bottle, but heck, its only noon.

"Jackson," I whisper, not wanting to startle him as I stand in the doorway.

He moves his head slightly as if he didn't hear me. A little louder, I ask, "Jackson, are you okay?"

His head pops up and he stares at me without saying a word. I can't place the look in his eyes.

"Say something, Jackson, you're scaring me."

"You came back?"

I shut the door behind me, walk over to his desk, push his chair away from the desk, and stand in between his legs.

"Of course, I came back."

"I'm sorry. I should have told you this was going on. I should have warned you so you would have known she was lying." He grabs my small shaking hands in his large strong hands. "I just thought the FBI would have gotten her confession sooner. They had the stupid druggie that beat her. It just took time to set up the sting to get her to say it."

"I'm sorry I didn't give you a chance to explain. Please don't hate me for that."

He stands framing my face with his hands. "Hate you? I could never hate you, Sunny, I love you."

I gasp in surprise. Jackson loves me. OMG, I love Jackson and he loves me back. The tears fall uncontrollably. I mutter through it and tell him what I wanted to tell him the last time we made love. "I love you too, Jackson."

He pulls my face to his and devours me in a possessive kiss. I can taste a hit of Crown on his lips, but mostly I taste Jackson. The unmistakable taste of my man. I lean my head back letting him own me. I wrap my arms around his neck and into his hair grasping for him. I want to make sure I have him—I need him.

"I need you," he says, looking down at me with eyes of desire.

"You have me."

His hands gather my dress and his skin is hot on my flesh. His hands feel so good as he caresses up and down my hips pulling my underwear down to my knees. "Get them off, Sunshine, I need you now."

Quickly, I jiggle out of them as I unbutton his shirt. I need to feel him as well. I rub my hands over his beautiful chest stopping over his heart and tiger tattoo. His heart is pounding as hard as mine, and it feels good to have him need me as much as a I need him.

"Look at me, Sunny. Promise me you will never run again."

"I promise," I say as I undo his belt buckle and release his pants. They fall to the floor where he steps out of them. I proceed to push his underwear down wanting to feel his need for me in my hands. I reach down grabbing his hardness, and it's pure hot steel. I stroke him hard and slow while looking into his eyes. He pulls my dress up and over my head, and then he unclasps my bra. Taking my nipple into his mouth, he finds my slick opening with his finger, plunging in hard and fast. I moan in pleasure.

He moves his kisses from my nipple up to my collarbone and then back up to my neck.

"I love you so fucking much, Sunny. I never want to be without you."

He pulls his cock out of my hands, lifts me up, and pushes me against the wall. I wrap my legs around his waist for support. He rubs his hard cock at my entrance, rubbing it up and down in my wetness like he always does. Looking me in the eye, he asks, "Move in with me tonight? I can't live another night without you in my bed."

He does not wait for a response, thrusting into me with exquisite pressure. He has one hand on the nape of my neck and the other around my waist supporting me. His thrusts in and out of me are hard and deep. I arch my back meeting his thrusts and trying to process what he has just asked me.

"Consider my bags packed because I don't want to live another night without you either," I pant.

He takes possession of my mouth again as he fucks me even harder. It's rough but loving I feel his need, his fear, and his relief. He plants his hands on the wall behind me as he hammers within me. Reaching down, I rub my clit. When Jackson groans, I explode into a million pieces trying to muffle my screams. He's right behind me as I continue to pump him by squeezing myself around him. He wraps me with his arms squeezing me tight.

Looking down into my eyes with sadness, he says, "I thought I lost you. I would rather go to prison than be without you."

"I'm here, and that crazy bitch is going to jail," I say, pulling his face to me with both hands and kissing his face all over.

Our mind-blowing office sex made us both very hungry. Jackson is in same condition I have been in. He has not eaten much in a while. The club doesn't open until later so we walk down Bourbon Street and slip inside Acme Oyster house.

"Have you ever had oysters?" Jackson asks, while we look over the menu.

I scrunch up my nose in disgust. "Oysters?"

He laughs and I drink in the sight of how handsome he is when smiling. His eyes shine as they watch my every move.

"You need to try them. They are a natural aphrodisiac."

"I don't think that's really necessary, do you? If we had any more sexual chemistry between the two of us, we would have to stay home twenty-four-seven. We would never get out of bed."

"And the problem with that is what?"

I smile at him thinking it actually sounds pretty good at the moment. At least for the next few days anyway. The waitress breaks my budding daydream asking what type of oysters we would like. The fear is written all over my face. I'm not sure I can do that.

In his husky smooth voice, Jackson orders for us. "I will have a dozen raw, and this beautiful lady will have a half-dozen chargrilled."

I raise one eyebrow at him, not knowing what I'm getting myself into. I'm grateful he isn't pushing me to try the raw ones. Moments later, the waitress returns with two trays. When she puts them down, the aroma of the garlic and butter is to die for. However, the look of Jackson's almost makes me nauseated.

"Come on, we will do it at the same time. You have that little girl fork for you to pick one up, and after I splash some hot sauce on here, I will suck mine down. Ready," he demands rather than asking. And I'm so head over heels for this man, if he said suck down a raw one, I would have to give it a shot. He picks his shell up and holds it up to his mouth while I fumble trying to get my little slick bugger out with this tiny fork.

"One, two, three," he says with raised eyebrows. And I do it. I shove it in and wait for the unknown. The flavors are amazing, lemon, butter, garlic, parsley, and it's just yummy. I open my eyes, not realizing I had squeezed them shut in anticipation. When I open them, Jackson has his hand on his flat belly laughing at me. "So it wasn't that bad, was it?"

"Actually, it was pretty good," I say, shoving the second one in. But I have to admit, watching him slurp the second one down really makes me a bit queasy.

The rest of our lunch is filled with talk of our future. I don't think I have ever planned a future with a man. It is so exciting!

"I have to admit, I can't say I'm sad you're quitting the club. I know a guy that works at Commander's Palace. He can hook you up with a waitress job while you go through school."

"Commander's Palace! I don't know, I have only been a waitress in a diner. I'm not sure I can do a fancy place like that."

"Babe, you have more class than anyone I know.

You'll do fine. I will give him a call tomorrow."

I tilt my head to the side still in amazement that I love this man and he loves me back. "I love you, Jackson Devereux."

"Back at ya, babe, I love you too," he says, reaching across the table and squeezing my hand.

"The waitress thing sounds great, but if I work days and you work nights, when will we see each other?"

"I'm quitting the club at the end of this week," he says, taking a big bite of his large hamburger.

"What? Why?"

"I only kept the job because you were there. Before you started, I had put some feelers out to local hotels for head of security, and yesterday, I got a call from the Ritz. They want me to start Monday."

"Oh Lord, Samantha is going to hate us."

"Nah, she's fine with it. That's how the strip club business goes. I've trained Sean from bartender to security. They will be fine."

Wow, the puzzle pieces are just falling together for me. It's so surreal. This has never happened to me; nothing ever goes the way it should for me. I almost feel like looking around to see when the rug will be pulled from under my feet.

"Stop daydreaming, Sunny. Everything is going to be fine. I see the worry on your face. I have no more secrets, and I will never let anyone hurt you, so forget about it."

I smile trusting he will forever keep me safe.

We walk back to the club hand in hand in utter elation. The air is cool outside but my heart is so warm.

"Where have you lovebirds been?" Samantha yells from the bar.

"Acme's. Jackson made me try oysters."

"Oysters. Shit, I'm gonna have to pay the cleaning crew extra to clean Jackson's office with y'all eating that shit."

Jackson grunts and walks away from us to let us chat. Samantha pulls me into another hug. She sure is touchy-feely lately.

"I'm so happy for y'all. Promise you will keep in touch. Jackson told me he's leaving so you won't have a reason to come back to see me."

"Carmella will be here."

"Girl, it's only a matter of time before a movie company scoops her up on me as well. And hell, I want her to move on. I mean really, I know my shit is fancy, but let's face it, it's still a strip club with a sex club pulling us along."

"Thanks for letting me into your work family. Without you, I wouldn't be here and this happy today."

"Actually, you need to thank Shelby. She pushed me to hire you," she says, smiling at me.

"Yes, you are right. Please let me know next time ya'll do lunch, and I would love to tag along."

She smiles big at my use of the word ya'll. "Will do, girl, now go kiss that hunk of man of yours goodbye so he can put his head in the game for the next two nights. You go soak in a hot bubble bath and be ready and waiting for his oyster-eating ass when he gets home."

I laugh and shake my head as I walk away from her heading to the back. I stick my head in Jackson's office. "Hey, handsome, I'm gonna run so you can get work done. I'm going to pack up the little bit of stuff I have at Carmella's."

"Sounds good. I will come crash with you tonight because it's gonna be late when I get off, and we'll head to my house in the morning, yeah?"

"Perfect." I reach into my purse and throw him my key. Carmella keeps a spare in the flowerpot outside the apartment I can use to get in.

"You're not gonna come give me a kiss goodbye?" he asks from his desk.

I blow him a kiss from the door. "You know as well as I do what will happen if I walk into that office," I say, raising my eyebrows at him. "And your shift starts in five minutes."

"I can be done in five," he says, getting up from his desk and striding to the door.

"Oh no, save your oysters 'til later."

He pulls me into his arms kissing me and deep pressing his hardness into my belly.

"Babe, you're gonna kill me if I have to wait 'til tonight."

"It will keep you alert and wanting." I smile and walk away, blowing him another kiss over my shoulder. I go to my locker to pick up my personal belongings. The only thing in here I need is my grandmother's necklace. The rest of the stuff is just costumes, and I don't need these. I hear the door to the dressing room open and see Dixie bounce in.

"Hey, girl, so I hear you are making it out of the stripping world," she says in a cheerful voice. I love these girls. She's not jealous I'm leaving. She's truly happy for me.

"Yeah, Jackson helped me get into college," I say, looking at the ground.

"Girl, look at me. Be proud, don't be ashamed. Hey, I know we don't grow up wanting to be a stripper, but hey, I'm really good with it. I make a shit load of money only working three to four hours a night. And this is the best establishment I've ever worked for. I have no complaints. And it gives me more time with my kiddos."

She wraps me in a hug, whispering into my ear, "But I'm going to miss you, so don't be a stranger."

Pulling back, I see her glassy eyes. "Don't worry, we'll make it a habit to have lunch once a month, I promise."

"Deal," she says, kissing my cheek.

CHAPTER 19

Sunny

I walk back to my apartment in a bubble of happiness ready to start the new chapter of my life. As soon as I hit the door, my phone goes off, notifying me of a text message.

Carmella:
Hey chick
My latest hookup set me up w/2
tickets to Maroon 5
@ House of Blues
U in?

Me:
What time?

Carmella:
9

Me:
Sounds good
Want me to meet u there?

Carmella:
Im gonna grab a taxi
fm the club pick u up @ 8:45
Be ready bitch bc Im
EXCITED

Me:
Me too
Sounds like fun

Carmella:
See ya soon

I start to pack the small amount of clothes I have accumulated in the four months I've been here. It doesn't take long before I'm done. I look at the clock on the wall to see it's only 6:00 p.m. I guess I better take a nap before my big night out with Carmella. And once Jackson gets home, I will need some extra energy to make up for lost time. I set my phone alarm to go off at 7:30 and lie down to rest. Today was an exhausting day, and I'm out in seconds feeling like I've slept for hours when the alarm goes off an hour and a half later.

I jump up, gather my clothes, and head to the shower. Looking down at my phone, I notice the battery is about dead. I plug it into the charger and throw it down on the bed. As I turn to make my way back down the hall to the bathroom, a sense of panic washes over me for no apparent reason. I stand still, listening to see if I hear anything and feeling like I'm being watched again. After a few deep breaths, I convince myself it's nothing. I tell myself that just because my world has been turned upside down every time things fall into place does not mean it will happen again.

I shut the bathroom door behind me and try to move into a happy place. The House of Blues is a pretty cool club, I hear. I have never been there. I jump in the shower and let the warm water soothe my tension.

Once I get out, I dry off and start to get dressed. Pulling on a pair of tight black jeans that hug my hips, I turn and look at how well Melinda's work has been done on my back. After she removed the tattoo, she started a new procedure that tattoos the color of my skin over the scar tissue from the removal. I can tell it was there because I know it was, but really, a stranger would not notice.

I smile seeing my reflection and the happiness in my

eyes. I think the weather is going to be pretty chilly tonight so I slip on a long-sleeved fitted T-shirt and a cute jean jacket Carmella and I found on sale during our Black Friday shopping. Putting on the last bit of light makeup, I realize I have no idea what time it is. "Geez I hope I'm not running late," I say aloud to myself and run back to my room to grab my purse and phone.

I see my purse first and fling it over my head and across my chest. I look for my phone but don't see it on the bed. That's weird, I thought I plugged it in here. Just as that thought crosses my mind, I hear a text message ping from the living room. Thinking I must have plugged it in there, I flip the light off and hurry to the living room hoping Carmella is not waiting outside in the taxi. She is very impatient; I would never hear the end of it.

As my feet hit the threshold of the living room, the light flicks on. My blood turns to ice and my feet fail me, as they have stopped working. I see the form in front of me and I may black out. My heart pumps so hard I can't hear, and my vision starts to blur as I brace my hands on the doorframe.

CHAPTER 20

Sunny

"What, no big smile for me, Mary?" Rex sneers.

He sits in the lounge chair next to the sofa under the lamp with my phone in his hand. *OMG, how long has he been here?*

"I hate to break the news to you, but you're going to miss your little concert tonight," he says, looking down at his watch. "Your little friend will be here in about fifteen minutes so we gotta run. Hope you enjoyed your time here because it's over," he says with so much evil and hate. "Actually, it's all over for you."

I know this is the end for me. I see it in his eyes, and they are dead and empty. He used to be reachable, but I can see he no longer has a soul left. There is no way out for me.

"This is how it's going to work. We are going to leave your phone here," he says as the phone hits the floor and is smashed by his large boot. "You won't need that anymore."

I feel the bile rise in my throat as I am frozen in fear. I still can't move. How did he find me? Why is this happening to me? How can I get away? I have to get away. I won't allow him to take my life here away from me.

"I see them stupid wheels turning in that little pathetic brain of yours. Forget about it. There's no way out for you. I thought we had this conversation back in that bathroom stall near Chicago. I told you what I would do if you ran again," he yells. "Fuck, Mary, why are you making me do this?"

Somehow I manage to speak. "You don't have to, Rex." But there is nothing I can say to try to get out of this. I can't tell him I love him, not even to try to get out of this. He would see right through it. I can only pray someone hears him screaming and calls the police before Carmella arrives.

"Oh, but I have to, Mary. You see, once you left me, they all turned on me. My own fucking men turned on me. I had to fucking shoot Tec three times before he would even give me the password to your trackers."

"Oh my God, is he okay?" I gasp, putting my hands to my chest and thinking I would be devastated if Tec died trying to protect me.

"What do you care?" he replies.

"They were like my family, Rex, I care." The pain in my heart is no longer panic but sorrow that I have put Tec in danger and possibly in his grave.

"Well, don't worry, he's alive and well and singing like a fucking canary to the FBI. I should have put the final bullet in him when he gave up the password, but I was too damn fixated on getting to you, and I left him bleeding on the floor."

"Why do you want me, Rex?" I ask with a shaky voice. "You know I don't love you, so why come for me?"

He takes two long strides to me, and I know what's coming. I brace myself against the wall for support. To my surprise, he doesn't strike me. Without opening my eyes, I know his face is millimeters from mine. He's so close I smell the stale smell of cigarettes and whiskey, which makes my stomach roll as his lips crash onto mine.

My hands instantly go up to his chest, pushing him away as hard as I can. This only angers him as he pushes his way into my mouth. I try turning my head away from his lips. Big mistake. He grabs my face with his large hands. I feel his thumb and fingers digging into my soft flesh knowing it will bruise. His tongue is invading my mouth with force and contempt. He uses the hand on my face to slam my head against the wall. My eyes fly open and all I see is hate. My heart stops when I see the flash of metal from the corner of my eye followed by the cold metal barrel pressed against my temple.

"Scream and I shoot you where you stand. I have nothing to lose. The FBI is on me, and it's only a matter of time before they find me. But I figured I could have a taste of you before I'm locked up."

The thought of him having me after having Jackson in my life makes me ill. It takes everything I have not to vomit in his face. I think I would rather him just beat me than put his hands on me.

"Stop daydreaming, Mary, and listen closely. We're going to walk out of this apartment and get into my truck. My gun will be under your jacket the entire time. Try to scream or run and I'll shoot you. Remember, I have nothing to lose. And if you don't want anything to happen to your dear friend Carmella, I suggest we get moving so I don't have to hassle with two bitches."

Oh God, would he really hurt Carmella? He shot Tec three times and that was his brother. Of course, he would hurt Carmella.

"Then let's go, Rex," I say with a surprisingly steady voice. I can't risk her life. I made my bed and I have to lie in it. She didn't choose this mess. I did. Hopefully he gets sloppy at some point and I can get away, but I can't risk having her hurt.

"That's my girl, let's go," he says, ushering me out the door and onto the street. His truck is illegally parked right in front of the apartment. He has his arm tightly around my waist with the other holding the gun and digging it into my side. He opens the door as if he's a southern gentleman making me get in on the driver's side. My heart sinks even further when I see he has removed the passenger side door handle. The windows are tinted so black that no one can see in, especially at night.

He slams the door and pushes my head down toward the passenger side so I'm lying on my belly. Terror rushes though me when I feel the cold metal of handcuffs around my wrist. He handcuffs my hands behind my back and then yanks me up cuffing a second set of cuffs to something he has rigged behind the truck seat.

A single tear falls down my face realizing I may never see Jackson again. He didn't just wake up today and find me. He has been following me for some time and he has a plan. That's when my gut tells me he is going to kill me. The nightmare that has haunted me is right here in front of me. The thought chills me to the bone, and I start to shake uncontrollably.

"Quit being a fucking baby, Mary. How could you not know I was coming for you? I told you I would. Oh yeah, you thought you were smart enough, didn't you? I have to admit, putting your clothes in those damn train cars was brilliant. I had my men fan out all over the fucking country."

He pushes my hair behind my shoulder as I whimper in fear. Licking my ear, he continues, "You see, your problem is, you thought I would stop looking. But I never did. It took me three months and twenty-seven fucking days to track you down. With your clothes all over the damn country, I had to figure out which one was really you," he says, sliding his gun under my grandmother's heart locket. "You see, Mary, when I had your precious locket cleaned, I had that bugged too."

"How could you?"

He chuckles, "How couldn't I is the real question. I knew you were too good for me, but I don't care. You're mine. Thank God, you love your grandmother too much to let the necklace go because she led me straight to you."

"You fucking bastard!"

"Oh, Mary, don't get sassy with me. It won't do you any good," he says, looking at the road and putting the truck in gear. As he pulls away, I see a taxi pull up and Carmella gets out. I pray he doesn't know it's her. He doesn't flinch, and we are out on the road with her out of danger. I watch her in the mirror jogging up the walk the door.

How in the hell am I going to get out of this? Come on, Sunny, think.... ... I have to make it through this; I have to be with Jackson. I won't allow Rex to take away my happiness. I will have to fight for my life to stay alive.

I try to pay attention to where we are heading in case I can make an escape. Meanwhile, I have to talk to Rex and try to calm him down and bring out the man he was before he was president of The Flaming Dragons.

"Rex," I say softly. "You don't have to do this." He doesn't respond but I see his jaw clench. "I will always love you, Rex, love you for what you did for my grandmother. Love you for the man you used to be."

He shifts his eyes to me momentarily. "It's too late for that, Mary. I was never that man I made you believe I was." His voice sounds strained. "Don't you get it? I always knew I was going to be the MC president, but twinkies and skanks didn't do it for me. I wanted a fresh pussy, one that had never been touched by my brothers. And when I saw you at that strip club so young and innocent, I knew you were what I wanted. And once I tasted that sweet pussy of yours, I knew from that second I would never let it go. And Mary, I ain't letting it go. You're mine for life, and if our lives end tonight, so be it but you're mine."

"What if I say I will go with you and be with you?" I ask, lying through my teeth and hoping to buy more time.

Without looking at me, he responds, "I would know you were lying."

Those words send chills through me. There's nothing I can tell him to stop him from the path he is set on. I focus back on the road to see we're now on the interstate and moving quickly away from the city and out of the state. I think we're headed to Mississippi but I'm not sure yet.

"You see, Mary, you can't talk your way out of this. I have accepted the fact that you hate me and that you would never really surrender to me like I want you to. Because the truth is, I want your pussy but with a skank's brain. I wanted you to know your place as an old lady and to train you to suck me off any time any place.

I grunt out loud thinking he must be out of his mind. I would have never had sex with him in the clubhouse in front of everyone.

"But since that was never, and will never be, an option, and I'm a wanted man by the FBI now, the gig is up for me. And since you're the reason my brothers turned on me, it's only fitting I get my last taste of you before we both call it quits."

My chest hurts so bad when I hear his words. They're laced with pure evil spewing out of him like a faucet. He continues with his visions of what he will do to me and how he will let me die. My hands are handcuffed behind my back, and there's nothing I can do. The truck barrels down the interstate at ninety miles per hour. *Please, God, let us get pulled over.* That's my only hope. I resolve to simply pray for a miracle as we drive.

CHAPTER 21

Samantha

I sit at my desk trying to figure out the new schedule without Sunny and Jackson. Knowing Parke is a police officer, I will move him up to head of security for now. I know that will piss people off because he is just a bartender, but Sean is not ready. I will let them all know I don't give a shit what they think. Parke has years of military experience, and I'm doing what's best for the club. Hell, they don't like it, they can leave too.

My cell phone rings and I see Carmella's face come across the screen. "Please tell me you are not quitting? I can't take three in one week."

"Samantha, something terrible has happened to Sunny. I need Jackson, but he's not answering my calls."

I hit the speaker on my desk phone and buzz Jackson's earpiece. "Yeah."

"Jackson, I have a problem. I need you in my office stat."

"How serious is your problem because I have—" "It's Sunny. Something's wrong and I need you in my office—" and the line goes dead.

I go back to my cell phone. "Jackson is on his way to my office. Tell me what is going on."

"Fuck, I think that bastard found her."

"Who?"

"Rex the MC guy that beat the shit out of her, the reason she's hiding out here."

"MC guy, what does that mean?"

"motorcycle guy."

"Oh God …"

"What? That doesn't sound good."

"I don't have time to discuss it. Tell me what you see that makes you think he has been there."

"I came home to pick her up, but she wasn't waiting outside. I ran in and the door handle was taken off the front door, and her cell phone is on the ground smashed in a million pieces," she gasps and starts to sob into the phone.

"It's okay. We're going to find her. Get back in the cab and come straight here."

"Okay," she says, out of breath and hangs up.

My door flies open and Jackson barges in. "What's wrong with Sunny?"

"Carmella just called and said Sunny was supposed to meet her outside the apartment and when she got there no one was there. Jackson, the doorknob was removed and her cell phone was left there smashed to pieces."

"Fuck, how could he find her? Did you call the police yet?"

I pick up the phone and dial Parke's number. "Hey, it's me. I need you in my office now!"

Of course, his comment is off color, as he has no clue how serious this is. "Parke, NOW. Sunny is missing, and from what Carmella is telling me, the ex she has been running from is in a motorcycle gang."

"On my way," he grunts into the phone right before the line goes dead.

"Why the fuck are you wasting your time with your boyfriend the bartender and not the cops?" Jackson says, pushing me aside to get to the phone.

"He is a cop," I say for the first time out loud. "He has been working here undercover. First it was to see if this was a whorehouse, and when that didn't pan out, his job was to look for a motorcycle guy from St. Louis."

"I'm the head of fucking security, and you don't think that information was important enough to tell me?" I jump as he slams his fist down on my desk in anger. "How do you expect me to protect her if I don't know what the hell is going on?"

"Jackson, I had no idea her ex was in a motorcycle group. I'm sorry, she never shared that with me and I didn't want to pry. And we don't even know if we are talking about the same groups here."

Parke comes rushing in. "Details, facts," he demands. I give him the info we know and he turns to Jackson. "Do you know what MC club he was in?"

"The Flaming Dragons. He is the president," Jackson says in a tight tone. He is clenching and unclenching his fists while a large vein bulges in his neck.

"Thank fuck," Parke says, earning a very deadly look from Jackson. "Apparently, Samantha has told you I'm with the NOPD undercover, yeah?"

"Get to the fucking point. My girl's in danger."

"Long story short, we knew Rex was on his way down here, but we didn't know he was after anyone. To our knowledge, the Bayou Bandits were going to give him cover for the shit that was coming down on him in St. Louis from the FBI. Running guns, drugs, and attempted murder on one of his own. His own brothers turned him in."

"So why in the fuck is this good news?"

Parke does not answer him right away, turning and pulling out his phone and dialing. Jackson is losing patience fast, and if Parke doesn't answer him soon, I can see we're going to have a problem.

Parke looks up at Jackson as he starts to speak on the phone. "Yeah, this is Lieutenant Boudreaux. I'm sending you the link to my trace, and I need backup following it. The subject I've been tailing is on the run, and he has kidnapped a twenty-one-year-old female. Yeah ... Yeah ... put every Goddamn thing you got on this. I'm leaving the club now to follow the tracking device," he says, hanging up. "I put a tracker on his truck three days ago. He has been snooping around here, but I assumed it was to hang with the Bandits."

"Well, let's get the fuck out of here," Jackson yells,

walking out the door and expecting Parke to follow him.

I look up at Parke with pleading eyes. "Please go find her, hurry!" He kisses me quickly and runs out the door. I follow him and yell behind him, "Be careful." I sit back at my desk feeling helpless as I put my head in my hands and cry for the first time since Phillip's death.

Carmella's voice pulls me out of my worry, "Where is everyone? What's going on? Parke and Jackson about ran over me in the parking lot."

I jump up from my desk and wrap Carmella in my arms holding her tight. "They're going to get her. Thank God, Parke put a tracker on the guy's truck three days ago so they should be able to find her pretty quickly."

She pushes back giving me a confused look, "Parke? Why would he do that? And how did he know about Rex? Sunny only told Jackson and I."

I give her the rundown just as two uniformed officers knock on my door asking to speak to Carmella. She gives them her statement and even recalls seeing the black truck with dark tinted windows pulling away from their apartment, giving them the exact time Sunny was taken.

Carmella and I can only sit and wait to hear something from Jackson and Parke. It is pure agony.

CHAPTER 22

Sunny

Lord, when will he stop driving? I'm not sure I want him to because I know what he will do to me when he does. As if he is a mind reader, we pull off the interstate and start down a long dark road. I saw a sign that said we're in Biloxi, Mississippi now. After a few minutes down this road, we pull up to a shack on the side of the road. I'm sure at one time it was a house, but it looks like a rundown shed now. There were no other homes on the road so no one will even hear me scream. My legs start to quiver when the engine shuts off.

He turns to look at me and the only thing I can see is the Devil. "It's party time, Mary." He smirks and pulls me out of the truck through the driver's side by the handcuffs. Once I get to my feet, he keeps a tight grasp on my arms and leads me to the shack. He flings the door open and the stench of mildew hits me. When he pushes me further into the room, I hear the door lock behind us at the same moment the light comes on. It's a small lamp that does not throw off much light. Thank God, because from what I can see, the place is filthy. It's a one-room shack with a bed on one side of the room and a kitchen table and chairs on the other. There's a tiny apartment fridge and a small TV. The front windows facing the street have been blacked out with what looks like black spray paint, and the back windows are covered in old orange drapes.

The fear really sets in when Rex pushes me up against the wall and puts his lips on my neck. "This won't be short and sweet so get used to it." His breath is hot and disgusting on my neck. "But I need a drink first." He pushes me down against the bed cuffing the cuffs to the bedpost. "I don't want to hear your whining voice unless I ask you to scream my name when I come, understand?"

I look around for any possible way out. A silent tear slips down my cheek as I come to the realization there is no way out. He does not trust me, and if I don't get out of these cuffs, I'm done. I sit and watch Rex drink from the whiskey bottle as he watches me with contempt.

After what seems like hours, Rex has finished more than half the bottle. He has not said one word to me the entire time, and I don't dare speak to him. He gets up from the table, walks over to me, and un-cuffs me from the bed. "Get up," he slurs, "I said, get the fuck up."

I get up as quickly as I can when he pushes me face first into the wall with a thud. I was able to turn my head fast enough not to break my nose, but the pain I feel in my hip startles me. When I look down to the radiating pain, I see my purse is still hanging across my chest over my hip. I almost break out into a panic when I remember I have it. He didn't even ask me about the purse or what I have in it. *Thank you, Jackson for making me go to the shooting range and making me get a concealed weapons permit. And most of all, my handsome man, thank you for buying me a very small girly gun,* I yell inside of my head. *But how in the hell am I going to get to it?* My hands have not been free since the moment I saw him in my living room.

Rex unbuttoning my jeans pulls me out of my plan. "What the fuck?" he yells as his fingers dig into my back where his tattoo once was. "You think it's that easy? You think you can just remove me like that?"

He now has his hand fisted in my hair pulling my head back. "Oh, bitch, you are going to pay for removing that tat, you hear me?"

"I'm sorry, Rex, whatever you want. I'll give you whatever you want."

His grasp tightens, and I don't know how my hair has not just been pulled out by the roots. My eyes are closed, but I smell the whiskey getting stronger, and his lips are on mine as he pushes his body flush against mine. His front is to my back, and I feel his erection pressing against my ass as his tongue invades my mouth.

Opening my eyes, I see he has left his gun next to the bottle of whiskey on the table across the room, yet I feel cold metal on my back and freeze in terror. He has a knife and the blade is lightly running over my lower back where he had branded me with his symbol and name. "I think I should just carve my name right here. What do you think, Mary?"

"Please don't, Rex, I love you," I whisper. It feels so wrong, but I have to try and soften him.

He chuckles out loud, "You fucking love me, tell me another lie."

"Rex, I do love you. I always have loved you. You don't want to do this. Someone will look for me." That was not the right choice of words.

"Who is going to look for you, Mary?" he snarls. "You don't have anyone, or do you?" The blade moves from my back and down over my hip. The loud rip of the knife slicing thorough the seam of my jeans shakes me to the core. I don't have much time.

"Tell me, Mary, you have been giving my pussy away?"

I shake my head in denial as best I can with my face still pressed up against the wall. "No, Rex, but I have become close with the girls at the club, and they will look for me."

He roars with laughter, "You think those skank strippers give a shit about you. If that's the case, I have forever with you because no one is looking for you." He spins me around with the knife at my throat. "We're going to have a good time tonight, Mary, and when I'm tired of hearing you scream, it will all be over." He bends his head down and licks down my neck to pause at my breasts causing me to shiver in disgust. The blade follows his tongue and slides under my breasts. I do my best to stop my body from trembling, but his eyes are so dark and hollow, I know the Rex I once knew is no longer there.

He looks up at me pulling my breasts out of my bra and over my shirt squeezing them with his palm so hard I see stars. "Oh, did that hurt, baby?" he growls, slicing across my collarbone. I gasp in pain but don't scream out knowing that he wants it to hurt. I feel blood trickle down my breasts as he shoves me down to the floor. "Sit there. I need more to drink."

He walks away from me to the table. I had pulled my arms under my butt ignoring the slicing pain caused by the pulling of the cuffs. I rest my head on my knees to hide my hands under my legs. As I look down, I see both wrists are bleeding, but I ignore the pain and focus on trying to get them over my feet so I can reach my purse on my hip.

Rex slams the whiskey bottle down and starts to pace in the kitchen area while rambling. He looks like a mad man running his hands through his hair and pacing back and forth.

"It's all your fault. Do you know that?" he rants, turning away from me. "Why did you have to question me in front of my bothers? Why?" he shouts with his fist landing on the wall putting a hole in the sheetrock. Lucky for me, he is still turned away. I manage to get both feet out and my hands into my lap, but he doesn't notice. He just keeps yelling. *Thank God for the dim lighting.*

"Do you know how close I have been to finding you? Fucking Mardi Gras fucked it all up. I was within twenty-five feet of you at a parade but could not find you because they had so many fucking people. Then you were always heading out to a fucking swamp. Do you know there is no Goddamn cell coverage in the fucking swamp? I would lose you every time you went there," he yells, turning back to the bottle and downing the rest.

My heart pounds so loud I'm sure he can hear it. My hands shake as I try to open the flap of my purse while keeping my eyes on Rex. I finally get my hands on the gun, and I know what I have to do. There is no other option at this point.

Just as I get my hands on the gun and fingers threaded through the trigger, he turns around. I see fear flash in his eyes for a millisecond before rage fills them. He lunges for his gun, and the rest seems to move in slow motion but too fast to think.

The first bullet goes off and the sound is deafening. I don't even hear the second or third go off, but I see the smoke trail leave the barrel and then the pain kicks in. I feel the roar of my screams but there is no sound.

CHAPTER 23

Jackson

Parke and I jump into his Camaro and take off. He tosses me his phone. "The red dot is her. Give me directions, and we'll get to her, man, I promise."

I look down at the phone as he flips on the blue lights and we take off. "Fuck, man, they're already on I-10 headed to Mississippi almost past the last Louisiana exit."

"Okay, about how far ahead of us are they?"

"About a fucking hour. Is this the fastest you can drive?" I yell, looking over at the speedometer. "Come on, man, this fucking car has more than that. He's gonna kill her, you do know that? If we don't get there, he is going to kill her."

He looks over to me, and knowing I'm right, he shifts gears pushing the car to its limits. "Man, I had no idea he was looking for Sunny or anyone for that matter. He shot up one of his brothers when a deal went bad, and they ratted him out to the FBI for drugs and weapons trafficking," he continues with his eyes pinned on the road navigating us through the narrow New Orleans streets as we desperately try to make our way to the interstate. That's where we'll make up the time.

"Fuck, why didn't I know that?" He pounds his hand on the steering wheel in frustration.

"So what are we looking at when we find him? What charges is he running from? Ten years, twenty? What?" I ask.

Parke's expression doesn't change. We reach the interstate and he speeds up to 110 miles per hour now. He shakes his head and I know it's bad. "Fucking life, dude, he's looking at fucking life in the pen with no parole?"

"He's been at it awhile and he's selling to the Mexican

Cartel."

"Maybe he can cut a deal?"

He looks over from the driver's seat for a split second with a look that tells me we need to drive faster. "Nobody rats out on the Mexican Cartel if they want to live. He's looking at life with no way out."

I clench my fist in a ball and release it trying not to combust where I sit. I'm going to kill this motherfucker if he harms one hair on her head, I swear to it.

"Check the tracker. Where are they now?" Parke asks, bringing my attention back to the phone in my hand.

"We're gaining on them." As the words come out of my mouth, I see the tracker move off the interstate. "They got off in Biloxi. We are about thirty minutes behind them, maybe twenty at this speed."

The next twenty minutes are the longest twenty minutes of my life. Parke is now driving as fast as the car will take us as I watch the tracker sit still. My emotions are all over the place. I'm glad the tracker stopped but pissed as hell since he has her and is doing God knows what with her. We slow down to pull off the interstate and turn the lights off to avoid detection.

I pull my gun out and start tapping it on my leg anxious to get to her.

"Man, let me go in first. I have the badge," Parke demands.

I look at him with rage. If this motherfucker wasn't a friend and driving the car I'm in, I would have shot him for saying something so fucking stupid. "Fuck you, man, he's mine," I state without hesitation. I assume he senses I'm not going to budge so he lets it go.

The street is so fucking dark we have to slow down to a crawl on the gravel road that takes us to her location on the phone. As we pull in, my heart races when I see the black truck Carmella described. Parke stops the car and instincts kick in. We move quietly giving hand signals to each other. Approaching the house, my world stops and I know at that moment I've lost her when I hear three consecutive gun blasts. I take off running and kick in the front door afraid of what I will find.

The dim light hits my eyes, and I see her covered in blood. It takes me a second to realize she's still alive and the motherfucker is lying at her feet face down. I run over to her to inspect her body. Her eyes are open, but she's in shock with her gun still clasped in her hand.

Thank God, I showed her how to shoot and bought her this gun, thank fucking God!

"Where are you shot, Sunny?" I ask, while looking over her for wounds.

She looks up into my eyes. "You came for me?" she yells.

"Of course, I came for you. Now give me the gun, babe," I say softly, removing the gun from her hands. I see Parke checking the scum bag for a pulse, and I look up at him. "He's done?"

"Yeah," he responds, pulling out his cell phone to call in the uniforms.

I pick Sunny up and lie her on the dirty bed knowing she has to be hit somewhere with the amount of blood on her. She pulls my shirt trying to pull me to her with her hands still handcuffed. "I'm okay, Jackson, hold me please."

"I will babe, but I have to see if he hit you."

"He never got a shot off," she says as I pull her back to look at her face. "Thank you for teaching me to shoot. I hit my target all three times." She's trembling hard now, and I want to get her the fuck out of here. Her voice is shaky when her beautiful green eyes look up at me. "He kept coming at me even though I was shooting. I lifted the gun and fired the third round which hit right in between his dead evil eyes." She motions to all the blood on her. "That's what this is. I'm not hurt. It's all from him," she cries. "I want to go home, Jackson, please take me home."

"Shhh." I pat her head as she lays it on my chest. "As soon as the uniforms get here and take your statement, we'll get you home." She quiets down but her grip on my leg by her restricted hands tightens like she never wants to let go. And I don't want her to. She's mine.

I take my shirt off to wrap it around her waist as her jeans have been ripped to shreds. It feels good to have her back in my arms. Her soft shaky hand runs over my tiger tattoo and her eyes grow wide. "She said the tiger would save me from the dragon, Jackson."

"Who, baby?"

"The Voodoo Queen," she says and smiles.

"Well, babe, she was wrong because you saved yourself," I reply.

She shakes her head and brings her lips up to mine. "Without you, I would have never had a gun in my purse, much less know how to shoot it." Her lips touch mine and she whimpers in relief as we kiss.

The paramedics finally make it here, and I have them check her out anyway. They bandage up the nasty cut on her collarbone, cut the cuffs from her wrists, and take care of the cuts the cuffs dug into her flesh.

She gives her statement and we are on our way. It didn't take long for them to realize Rex was a piece of shit, and Sunny did them a favor when all was said and done. Gotta love the good ole boys in blue down south. No one will miss him, look for him, or care he's dead. I have to admit, it enrages me that I could not put my hands on him and make him suffer first. But I'm proud of my girl and glad she did what she had to do to stay alive. Sunny didn't realize it, but Rex did get a shot off. It just didn't hit her. The hole was right above her fucking head.

The sun shines through the curtains while I watch the rays dance on her face. I have not slept yet since getting back from Mississippi. My adrenaline is through the roof, and the thought of losing her has me so worked up I don't want to take my eyes off her.

The events from last night play over and over in my mind. After getting home, I had bathed her and checked over her body again to ensure he didn't touch her. I knew from training not to ask her questions right away and that fucking killed me. I wanted to know if he had touched what was mine. Did he put his filthy hands where she didn't want him to? Once I had her cleaned up and wrapped tightly in my arms lying in bed, she had whispered to me, "He put his hands and mouth on me, but he didn't get a chance to do what he wanted to me, Jackson."

"Shh, it's okay, babe, we don't need to go over this now."

Turning in my arms, she kissed my tattoo. "I just want to let you know I'm still yours and he didn't ..."

I put my finger on her lips. "It doesn't matter what he did. I love you no matter what."

She kissed my finger, sucking it into her mouth and releasing when I growled, "Then make love to me, Jackson, I need to feel you still want me. That his hands on me don't matter because I didn't want them there."

In one swift move, I had her on her back and I hovered over her with my hips positioned in between her legs. "Don't for one second ever think I don't want you. I don't only want you, I NEED you," I stressed. "Without you, my world is nothing, I can't breathe without you."

I saw the joy in her eyes hearing my words. Without asking permission, I pushed into her steady and hard watching her beautiful eyes roll back in her head as she arched her back off the bed.

"Oh, Jackson, please?"

"Please what, babe, tell me what you need."

She opened her eyes and dug her nails into my ass pulling me toward her. "I need you to not be gentle. I want to feel your passion. I want to know I'm alive."

I gave her what she needed pounding into her harder and feeling her pussy tighten around my cock with every push. I fucking love this woman and I don't want to ever be without her. I heard her breath quicken and felt her clenching around me she was so close. I slowed down but pulled all the way out before pushing back in.

"Oh, Jackson," she moaned.

"Babe, I love when you moan my name."

I leaned down and sucked up her neck until I reached her ear while still pushing slow, hard, long thrusts in and out of her warm wet pussy. Reaching up, I found her nipple and twisted it lightly just enough to tease her but not push her over. Looking down at her, I said, "Marry me, Sunny, I don't want to ever be without you again."

A smile spread across her face while a tear slipped down her face but she didn't speak. I tightened my grip on her nipple as I saw her retreating into her head. She lifted her hands and framed my face. "I don't want to ever be without you either, Jackson. Tell me when and where, and I would be honored to marry you."

I smashed my lips onto her and lost control of my slow pace and pushed her into bliss falling right along with her.

As the night replays in my mind, she opens her eyes and smiles at me watching her.

"Good morning, handsome," she says, making my dick twitch again.

"Good morning, sunshine."

She snuggles her glorious naked body against mine letting her hand fall to my cock and rubbing it up and down. After just a few strokes, I'm as hard as steel wanting her again. Before I can move, she is on top of me looking down at me.

"I love you, Jackson, and I can't wait to be your wife."

Her eyes don't leave mine as her sweet wet pussy slowly slides down my cock. My fingers grip her hips and she starts to move. The only thought that runs through my mind right now is how fucking awesome forever will be with this woman.

EPILOUGE

6 months later - Sunny

I sit out on the back deck letting the rays warm my skin while the sight of Jackson throwing crab traps into the bayou warms my heart. It has been a rough six months coming to terms with the fact that I had to take Rex's life to save my own. But with counseling, I've learned to let myself live life to the fullest, letting go of the guilt and knowing I would be in the grave had I not pulled the trigger.

I smile at the thought of where my life is today and where it's headed. I started college a few weeks ago, which has taken some time to get used to being back at school and doing homework, but our lives have fallen into a wonderful routine. And I say our lives as Jackson and I are engaged. I raise my hand looking down at the sparkling diamond and thinking of Jackson down on one knee in front of the Cathedral proposing and professing his undying love to me. I can't ever imagine my life without him and know I will never have to.

My phone buzzes forcing me to pull my eyes away from Jackson's bare chest. Looking down, I see it's Carmella.

"Hey, bitch, what's up?" I ask, giggling.

"You know, I think I have rubbed off on you too much, bitch."

I smile into the phone from ear to ear feeling the love we have for each other. She is truly like a sister.

"Yes, you have. Now what do you want? I'm busy here watching my sexy fiancé throw crab traps. Do you know how fucking sexy this man is when he does that?"

She makes a gagging sound. "You two are sickening, When is all that lovey-dovey stuff going to fade?"

"I hope never. Don't be a hater, girl, you will find your man one day."

I hear her huffing into the phone, "Well, I don't know about a man, but I found a new job?"

"You are leaving Samantha," I gasp.

"Yeah, I feel bad, but I can't pass this up. I had a movie producer approach me about doing the makeup for a movie being filmed here in New Orleans. The pay is $250K a year. Did you hear me? That is crazy shit. How can I pass that up?"

"Well, you can't. I'm sure Samantha will understand. And you do know she always knew this day would come. She told me the day I interviewed that you would get a better offer one day and she would have to let you go. But at least you will still be in New Orleans. I would die if you had to go to Los Angeles."

"Well …"

"No, you can't leave me."

"I'm not leaving you, and you have Jackson. What do you need me for anyway?"

"You're my sister. I will always need you."

"This movie will be here for about six months then the location will move, and I will go where it goes. I will always live in New Orleans, but if the movie is in Paris for two months, I will be in Paris for two months."

"I'm proud of you, Carmella. Follow your dreams. I know you will always come home."

"Girl, you know I will. Hey, we still on for our girls' night Friday, right?"

"Of course, why?"

"Because I can't wait to tell you how the interview of this job went. It was fucking CRAZY," she yells into the phone.

"Oh no, tell me now. I can't wait."

"Sorry, this is an in-person conversation. Let me run. I have shit to do."

"Love you, Carmella."
"Love you too, Sunny, see you on Friday."

ABOUT THE AUTHOR

The New Orleans Temptation Series is my debut series as an Indie Author. Hidden is book tow of the three part series. Devastated is the first book and can be read as a standalone so please check it out and go on a sensual journey with Shelby and Grant.

Devastated no on Amazon!

Living the American Dream Shelby had everything she could have dreamed of. A handsome husband two wonderful children a beautiful home and a great job. What else could she ask for?

In an instant her world is turned upside down when she innocently looks at her husband's phone. With this Devastating discovery Shelby has to decide if she will walk away from twenty years of marriage or will she find a way to fit into Grant's erotic world?

Will she walk on the wild side she never knew she had? How far will she go? If she crosses the line will she be able to live with herself when the sun comes up? Or will she let her over conservative personality end her marriage?

Find me on Facebook @ Monica May to find out when the final book of The New Orleans Temptation Series will be released.